"I'm not proud of what happened last night."

Lee spoke the clipped words as Kelsey's arms tightened around her. "I—I wasn't myself."

"No," he jeered, "you were human last night. You reacted like a normal woman when a man makes love to her—until your corporate lover called. Do you let the ice melt when you're in bed with him?"

Lee's head snapped up. "Not all men have your uncivilized animal instincts!"

Kelsey's lips quirked. "I bet he's never even asked for the privilege of sharing your bed. Does he make love to you at all? Does he kiss you?" he pursued with a sickeningly persistent curiosity.

"Why should that bother you?" she spat out angrily.

"Because I hate to see a good woman go to waste."

ELIZABETH GRAHAM

madrona island

Harlequin Books

TORONTO • LONDON • LOS ANGELES • AMSTERDAM
SYDNEY • HAMBURG • PARIS • STOCKHOLM • ATHENS • TOKYO

Harlequin Presents edition published August 1981
ISBN 0-373-10446-4

Original hardcover edition published in 1981
by Mills & Boon Limited

CHAPTER ONE

An immaculately manicured nail pressed down on the intercom button after its discreet buzz, and the secretary's voice, sounding more breathy than normal, filled the room.

'A call for you, Mrs Whitney, on line one. A Mr Kelsey Roberts.'

The pink-coated nail pressed momentarily harder on the black button before the cool voice, carefully modulated, said with its normal calmness, 'Tell Mr Roberts that I'm in conference right now. He can leave a message.'

'But he's——' Ruth dithered uncharacteristically, 'Mr Roberts has to leave in a few minutes to take his flight back to Seattle.'

'That's his problem, not mine,' was the cool reply. 'Tell him I'll be pleased to answer any letter he cares to write once he's back in Seattle.'

Lee Whitney turned her attention back to Maitland Frasier, who sat at comfortable ease at the other side of the ebony desk. Yet for a second or two it wasn't Maitland's pink, well-cared-for face that she saw, but the lean dark features of the man she had summarily dismissed on the telephone. Were Kelsey Roberts' features still hawklike in their prominence of high cheekbones, hollowed cheeks and thrusting, well-moulded chin? Or had the seven intervening years added the fullness of prosperity to the hungry leanness of his face, the rapier thinness of his body?

'It wouldn't hurt to talk to him,' Maitland suggested, his light blue eyes unsuspicious as they met the more vibrant azure of hers across the desk. 'He might be willing to pay a good price for the Frantug area of our operations. The tug business, as you know, is the least part of our operation now.'

True. Whitney Enterprises had moved up and away from its early beginnings as San Francisco's major supplier of tugs to the international shipping docking there. Now they were involved in diverse areas of business—imports from the Orient, the canning and marketing of Treeripe orange and grapefruit juice, even the well-established vineyards of Gappozzi, acquired upon the death of the family's last male member. Under Lee's shrewdly capable management, Whitney Enterprises had soared into areas Fletcher Whitney, her dead husband, had never dreamed of. A chain of neighbourhood markets in predominantly poorer areas where prices were geared to a reasonable level, the produce fresh and attractively presented, the staff handpicked for their ability to relate to the public they served; real estate purchased just before the big boom of two years before; even controlling interest in a company of Merchant Bankers.

Lee sighed as a mental list of their holdings flashed before her. No, Fletcher would never have countenanced the bold moves she had made since his death five years before. He would have appreciated the idea of a conglomerate such as she had built almost single-handedly, but he would never have had the necessary foresight himself. And why would he? she questioned silently, her eyes misting in remembrance of the man she had married. He had been old then, sixty-three to her twenty, brought up in an age of caution, not given to gambling.

'Well?'

Maitland sounded amused, indulgent at her lapse into the privacy of her thoughts.

'Well—what?' She blinked back to reality, focusing again on his assured features, the body which would run to fat in years to come despite his regular visits to the Businessmen's Gym.

'Are we going to hear what this Kelsey Roberts has to offer for Frantug?' Maitland persisted, his brow furrowing in recollection. 'Wasn't he the guy who talked to Fletcher a few years back about buying Frantug on instalment? As I remember, he didn't have two nickels to rub together, and Fletcher gave him the brush-off.' He laughed with cruel disdain. 'At least you have to give this Roberts fellow points for persistence!'

Lee picked up the gold pencil placed neatly beside the message pad on her desk. Twisting it between her thumb and forefinger, she said without looking at Maitland, 'Things are different now. He doesn't have to offer to buy on instalments. He and his brother have built a respectable shipping business in Seattle.' She looked up sharply when Maitland gave a rich chuckle.

'You amaze me, Lee. Maybe that's why you're such a good businesswoman. You've already looked into his background and found out all you need to know about his business status, haven't you?'

Oh yes, she had looked into Kelsey Roberts' standing in the business community, had followed every step of his success over the past seven years. The seven long and barren years since. . . .

'Don't I always?' she mocked, resisting the impulse to smooth with her hand the still-immaculate tresses of her red-gold hair, fastened into a sleek chignon at the back of her head. 'Whitney Enterprises has never been taken for a ride yet under my direction, and I don't intend to let it happen now.'

'You're very efficient,' Maitland acknowledged, hesitating before going on, 'Is that why Fletcher——?' He broke off, for once showing embarrassment.

'Married me?' Lee supplied coolly. 'No, that isn't why Fletcher married me. I was just his secretary then, and I had no more idea of how a big business worked than a high school senior. When—Fletcher died, I had to grow up all in a hurry.'

'You were more than his secretary,' Maitland insisted, watching her covertly from beneath a bush of fair eyebrows. 'Even before your marriage, he wouldn't make a move without discussing it with you first.' Casually, he added, 'He and your father were friends at one time, weren't they?'

Lee returned briefly, 'They were old Air Force buddies, yes. That's probably why Fletcher gave me a job in the first place, but it had nothing to do with our marriage.'

Hadn't it? Even as Lee met Maitland's eyes levelly across the desk, she was aware of her own duplicity.

Would Fletcher Whitney have married his young, distraught assistant if an undying bond had not existed between him and her father? If he, Barnaby Todd and his wife Lisa, had not been killed in the small private plane Barnaby cherished?

'Well,' Maitland almost visibly shook himself like a golden labrador emerging from water, 'I'd better get moving on the labour disputes at the vineyards.' Levering his big frame from the chair, he looked enquiringly at Lee. 'Should I pick you up around seven-thirty?'

'What?' Lee stared blankly up at him.

'The opera,' he elaborated with a trace of impatience. 'Had you forgotten? It's the last of the season, so we should be there.'

Of course. Maitland was very conscious of what was expected of a socially prominent couple in a city where everyone had social obligations. Lee, as Fletcher Whitney's widow, was expected to be a patron of the arts, maintaining his family connections with San Francisco's elite.

'Yes, I—I'll be ready, Maitland. Seven-thirty.'

For a long time after he had left her sumptuously decorated office Lee sat staring straight ahead, oblivious to the genuine leather chairs of deep-seated comfort, the expensive art prints upon the walls. She didn't want to go to the opera with Maitland. She wasn't a true lover of the music, liking only the haunting familiarity of well-known pieces, not the modern composition of tonight's fare. With unerring insight, she knew that she wanted only to go home and spend the evening in a bloodbath of remembrance, an easy flickering into life of the hatred that had consumed her for years past.

Kelsey Roberts. . . .

The intercom buzzed. 'Your car is here, Mrs Whitney,' Ruth reported without inflection.

'I'll be right down.'

Borne smoothly up San Francisco's hilly streets in the discreet black of the Lincoln Continental driven by the impassive Santos, Lee pushed away the memories clamouring for attention. She wouldn't think about Kelsey Roberts tonight. God knew there had been enough of that seven years ago, when every waking and sleeping thought had centred around his darkly intense features, the haunting blackness of his eyes, the hungry ambition harboured in their jet depths.

The car swung smoothly into the gravelled drive of a house perched on a level overlooking the beginning twinkle of lights reflected from the harbour area below. Drawing up at the impressive white pillared portico, Santos turned to ask politely, 'Will you be needing me tonight, Mrs Whitney?'

'No, Mr Frasier will be picking me up later,' Lee told him, waiting as he expected her to do until he opened the rear door with a subdued flourish before stepping out with her long slender legs on to the smooth sweep of driveway in front of the house. 'You and Sarah can have an uninterrupted evening.'

'Thank you, ma'am. I'll be here to collect you as usual at nine-fifteen in the morning.'

The wide oak door yielded immediately to her touch, and Lee stepped into the spacious foyer, con-

scious not only of the spiral staircase leading to the
upper floor, or the myriad doors giving off the hall,
but of the well-ordered peace that descended like a
mantle round her shoulders. Round-figured, tart-
tongued Hannah Straight, the housekeeper who ran
the imposing residence on oiled wheels, met her as
usual at the door.

'There's a cocktail waiting for you in the library,'
she informed Lee with an air of disgruntled surprise,
as if the evening cocktail was something of an innova-
tion, although Lee couldn't remember the evening
when a shaker had not been placed in the male-
orientated library, a hangover from the days when
Fletcher had relaxed from the day's toils in his capacious leather armchair beside the ornate fireplace.

'Thanks, Hannah.' Lee moved further into the
hall, her long strides taking her in the direction of the
library when Hannah's grumbling comment came
from behind.

'A Mr Kelsey Roberts has called twice in the last
half hour,' she complained, adding expressively,
'Why men can't confine business to business hours
beats me! Anyway, he said it was urgent, and,' she
searched in the pocket of her capacious white apron
before producing a scrap of white paper, 'you've to
call him at this number the minute you get home.'

A dry ball formed in Lee's throat as she took the
paper from the housekeeper, but her stride towards
the library was just as purposeful when she said over
her shoulder,

'I've already told Mr Roberts that he can com-
municate by letter from Seattle, there's no urgency

about his business with me.'

No urgency! Lee's fingers trembled as she poured a generous measure of the Martini into a waiting glass. The urgency as far as Kelsey Roberts was concerned had been seven years ago. When his child had lain embryonically within her. When Fletcher Whitney, eminently respected businessman and wartime buddy of her father, had offered to marry her. Without strings. A platonic relationship between an elderly man and a girl who needed his protection.

Tears blurred the clear liquid Lee stared into, tears that took her by surprise because of their rarity in recent times. With a defiant gesture, she lifted the glass to her mouth and emptied it in one swallow, refilling it again as soon as her shaking hand could lift the iced shaker. For once she was grateful for the generous proportions of the prepared shaker.

Old-fashioned he might have been, set with age in his ways, but Fletcher Whitney had been a true blue gentleman of the old style. He had deeply loved the wife who had died, childless, after thirty years of marriage. Yet he had found room in his heart for his friend's daughter, knowing he would be laughed at for proclaiming the birth of a child from his young wife.

Brushing the tears from the emotionally deepened blue of her eyes, Lee emptied the shaker into her glass and paced restlessly to stand in front of the laid but unlit fire. She had loved Fletcher—not as a lover of her youthful physical charms, but as she might have loved the father who had been snatched from her so suddenly, finally. She had been a wife to him in different, more ephemeral ways, in the short year of their marriage. To his life she had brought lightness, youth, and an almost psychic sense of what was good business for the Whitney Company, as it had been known then.

The loss of her child in the fourth month of pregnancy had subtly altered their relationship. Whereas Fletcher had assumed that once the emergency had passed Lee would want the freedom given to other women her age, she had opted for the security of his steady, fatherly affection. At that time, she had had her fill of attraction of the senses, the quick rise of passion and its almost mindless drive towards satisfaction . . . a satisfaction fleeting in its short duration.

Then, and now, she hadn't felt the need for the Kelsey Roberts of this world, men who inspired dreams of eternal commitment, yet who in the long run regarded any woman as fair game if she would play along.

The phone rang distantly in the hall, and presently Hannah made her appearance in the library. 'It's that Mr Roberts again,' she delivered in disgruntled fashion. 'I gave him your message, but he insists on speaking to you.'

Insists? How Kelsey must have changed in the intervening years! Before, he had been taut, high-strung like an untried violin. Now it seemed he had acquired the confidence of a successful man of business, on an equal footing with the President of Whitney Enterprises. A woman President who, in his thinking, would no doubt be susceptible to his male charms.

'All right, Hannah,' she heard herself saying, 'I'll talk to him myself. It seems that's the only way to get rid of him once and for all.'

Her carriage was only slightly less graceful than normal as she crossed the thick carpet and went to the telephone extension on the leather-topped desk and waited for Hannah to switch through the connection. Her voice was coolly noncommittal as she held the blood-coloured receiver to her ear.

'Yes? This is Mrs Whitney speaking.'

There was a pause, as if the caller had found it necessary to re-orientate his thoughts. Then, 'It's very good of you to spare the time to talk to me,' the disembodied voice came, so familiar in its intonation that Lee's fingers tightened whitely on the receiver. Would her own voice be transmitted as distinctively as his had been? She made the preliminary motions of clearing her throat, then decided to let the disguising huskiness stay.

'Not at all, Mr—Roberts? Though your call is quite unnecessary, you could have stated your business in a lettter.'

'What I have to say would be better on a one-to-one basis,' he said with the tantalising drawl she remembered so sickeningly well. Strange how once it had had the power to shatter every atom of her composure! Now it had no more effect than the alien sight of a housefly, escaping the screens on doors and windows, that walked inquisitively across the bare desk top. 'What would you say to a vacation in Canada for a week or two?'

'Canada?' Lee echoed blankly.

'I own a place up there,' Kelsey went on, undeterred by her coolness. 'The climate's a lot more attractive there than in San Francisco in August.'

'I'd say you were out of your mind,' Lee snapped
viciously, momentarily losing her cool control. 'San
Francisco is my home in all seasons, and that's the
way I like it.' She drew a deep breath. Despite the
instant sharpness of her tone, she was sure Kelsey
wouldn't recognise her voice after the passage of all
those years. She had been young when she loved him,
shyly vulnerable, no connection with the diamond-
hard personality she had developed since, one that
made even seasoned businessmen quail when her blue
eyes regarded them frostily. 'It's out of the question,
Mr—Roberts. My plans are already made for the
month of August, and,' she allowed acidly, 'I've
already told you that any proposals you have regarding Frantug can be dealt with by correspondence, at
least initially.'

There was a silence, and she wondered if Kelsey
was cursing the haughty female who refused to talk
business with him face to face. Maybe he had thought
to soften her up by inviting her to his home in
Canada, sure that his indisputable charms would
sway her in the right direction.

'There's another matter I wanted to discuss with
you,' he went on with tight reluctance at last. 'A
business proposition, which I think might appeal to
you.'

'Oh?' Despite herself, Lee couldn't prevent the
quiver of interest his words aroused. Her acute sense
of commerce, fostered by Fletcher's unlimited en-

couragement of her business abilities, was impossible to subdue, even when it was roused by a man like Kelsey Roberts. 'What kind of proposition?' she parried.

'Imports, exports, based in Seattle and Vancouver, Canada,' he responded briefly. 'That's all I'm prepared to say until you've looked over the possibilities personally. A visit to those areas is worth more than a million letters,' he concluded with a dry barb.

'What kind of interest is being shown in this— enterprise?' Lee queried crisply.

'None at all at the moment. It's not generally known that the properties are available. As soon as it is,' he sounded quietly convinced, 'there'll be plenty of interest, I assure you. I'm giving you a chance to get in on the ground floor. The principal of the relevant company will be at Madrona Island in August. It would be good policy for you to be there at the same time.'

'Madrona Island?'

Kelsey's voice was noncommittal as he came back with, 'That's the island we own in Canadian waters.'

'We?'

'My brother and I are co-owners.'

Lee chewed at her lip thoughtfully. Apart from what might be a good business deal, there was a confrontation with a man who had done his best to ruin her life—had ruined it, to all intents and purposes. The hatred she bore for him deep within her was a festering sore that could never be lanced and cleansed in ordinary ways. Perhaps if she confronted him boldly, head on, he would be exorcised from her psyche, consigned to the oblivion he deserved. She was introspective enough to know that until that exorcism took place, she would be a bad bargain for any other man.

She reached for the appointment book, a replica of the one on her office desk, and leafed through the gilt-edged pages. There were few engagements for August, a month when most people vacated the city for less harassed surroundings.

'I can arrange things so that I have a week free from mid-month,' she offered briskly.

'Make it two weeks and we have a deal,' Kelsey told her, his voice sharpening to a hard edge which might have concealed anything from triumph to excitement. 'That gives me some leeway in arranging the principal's visit.'

How ridiculous business terms were at times, Lee reflected, any mention of 'principal' immediately bringing to mind the stern but kindly principal of her high school years ago. In business, however, there was no room for the levity that thought provoked.

'If he's anxious to sell,' she said sharply, 'then he'll fit in with my convenience.'

Kelsey returned smoothly, as if used to dealing with recalcitrant clients, 'Normally, yes. But in this case, we're the ones courting his pleasure. It's to our advantage to fall in with his wishes.'

We—our. A long time ago it might have meant something that Kelsey linked himself and her in such intimacy. Now it left her cold.

'Very well,' her business persona briskly replied. 'I'll leave two weeks free on the condition that fuller

details of the proposal are on my desk for considera-
tion no later than July the twentieth.'

'You'll have them.' His tone was brusque now, and
Lee felt herself bridling . . . a futile exercise because,
without further explanation, Kelsey put down his
receiver and effectively cut off the conversation.

Feeling strangely let down, Lee stared at the dark
red telephone for long moments after she had replaced her own receiver. What had she let herself in
for? A momentary impulse to savour the sweetness of
revenge? Lifting the Martini glass, she walked back
to the expensively rock-faced fireplace wall and
stared down at the unlit logs piled in the grate, clutching her glass but not drinking from it.

Would revenge be as sweet if she committed herself
to spending two weeks on Kelsey Roberts' territory?
The dream that had haunted her for the past six
years, a dream more completely enveloping than any
romantic fantasy could ever be, had always run along
a familiar line. Kelsey would come seeking a
favour—yes, perhaps his continued pursuit of Frantug—unaware that the President of Whitney Enterprises was the girl he had manipulated and used years
before. The difference now was that he would dis-
cover she was no longer the sweet young innocent she
had been then; that, thanks to Fletcher, she was a
woman of stature with the power to make or break
him. It was that dream which had fired her dedica-
tion of brains and energy to becoming the shrewd
businesswoman she was today. Fletcher had opened
up the opportunity and made her ascent quicker, but
the drive within her would have carried her to the top
sooner or later, she knew that without vanity.

The only flaw in these arrangements she had just made with Kelsey was that she was committed to spending two weeks in his company, a crashing letdown after her dramatic unveiling of her identity. Still, she didn't have to stay on this Canadian island any longer than it took to wring every drop of sweetness from their initial meeting. She might even prolong the visit for a few days, pretending genuine interest in the shipping deal. It would be added nectar for her to bow out of the negotiations just when Kelsey believed everything was sewn up. Let *him* do the explaining to the Seattle principal!

'Are you going to get changed, or are you going to the opera like that?' Hannah's sarcastic question shattered her thoughts.

'What? Oh, no, I was just going upstairs.'

Lee turned from the fireplace and set the untouched Martini down on a side table as she crossed the room. Glancing at her watch, she exclaimed, 'Heavens, I'll have to fly, I'd no idea it was so late!'

Hannah followed her partway across the elegantly appointed hall. 'Did you get rid of that Mr Roberts as you said?'

Lee scarcely halted her purposeful stride towards the stairs. 'Not for good and all—not yet, anyway,' she said over her shoulder, sensing rather than seeing the housekeeper's despairing shake of the head.

Hannah's hostility on her marriage to Fletcher had reflected the general opinion of San Francisco society—that Lee had married a man old enough to be her father for the transparent reason that she valued the assets more than the man. Two months of observing Lee's obvious affection for Fletcher had, despite the indisuputable fact of their separate rooms, elicited a grudging recognition from Hannah and the development of a fierce protectiveness as if Lee was the child the belligerent Hannah had never had.

Already stripping off her business suit as she entered the suite of rooms which had been hers for almost seven years, Lee went to the bank of closets in her spacious dressing room and selected, after speedy thought, a tasteful floor-length dress in dove grey. The colour dimmed the intense dark blue of her eyes, but it was a safe choice for the vaguely stuffy atmosphere of the Opera House.

She was downstairs when Maitland, his eyes taking in the discreet dress and understated jewellery encircling her neck and wrist, said,

'You look just right.'

If he noticed the small gesture of irritation his words provoked there was no sign of it as he followed Lee into the small morning room where Hannah was to serve them a light dinner. His big frame, fined down in black evening dress, dominated the small round table laid for two.

'I've been thinking about the Frantug deal,' he said after gallantly holding Lee's gilt-backed chair, pausing while Hannah placed cold consommé before them, going on when she had whisked out of the room again, 'If this man Roberts can come up with a good deal, we'll be well out of it. It doesn't return that much to the company, and we have all the problems of running it. I say let him have it, we can use the capital more profitably elsewhere.'

Another flash of irritation brought Lee's brows down in a slight frown, a fleeting displeasure when she reminded herself that Maitland really cared about the company. In fact, his main attraction for her was that he was more orientated towards business pursuits than amatory ones. The sexual part of him was constrained only slightly less than it was in herself. Why that should be she had never seriously questioned; all she knew and was grateful for was that he posed no threat to her inviolability, seeming to subscribe to her own philosophy of 'once bitten, twice shy.' *Had* Maitland been bitten once, as she herself had been? No, men had the advantage over women in that respect. The short, fierce burning of passion left no permanent mark on them, no necessity to nourish the tiny seed brought to life by that selfsame passion.

'I'll let you know what I decide about Frantug when I get back from Canada,' she told him, expecting and getting his astonished stare over a suspended soup spoon.

'When you get back from *where*?'

'Canada. Kelsey Roberts has asked me to spend a couple of weeks on his island there.'

'And you're going?' he asked incredulously. 'But— you never go anywhere! Why the sudden change?' His eyes narrowed suspiciously. 'Did you know this Roberts when he was here before?'

'Of course,' Lee returned coolly. 'I could hardly avoid him, he was in and out of Fletcher's office like a yo-yo, and he had to go through me to see Fletcher.' How easy it had been for him to get to Fletcher through her!

Maitland stemmed the words on his tongue when Hannah returned with fluffy omelettes, garden-fresh vegetables and individual green salads. But when she had retreated once more, he let go with un-characteristic venom,

'And on the strength of a casual acquaintance years ago, you've accepted an invitation to his home? Frantug must be more important to you than I thought!'

'Frantug isn't, no,' Lee conceded. 'But he has an-other deal in mind, one I have to be there to look over personally—an export-import company out of Seattle and Vancouver. It could be a good deal for Whitney.'

'Then I'll come with you,' Maitland said trucu-lently, attacking the featherlight omelette before him with all the ardour of a steak man.

'No!' Lee said sharply, shading her voice to a softer tone as she added, 'I don't want Roberts to get the idea that it's that important to us. That—or Fran-tug.'

With no more than a few additional reinforcing phrases from her, Maitland grumblingly agreed that she should travel alone. Whatever had caused his previous aversion to her going alone was submerged in the acuteness of his business sense. Hardly flatter-ing to her in a personal way, but then her affection for Maitland, if it could be called that, was based on just that quality.

The rest of the evening was bland, conducive to the thought channels she normally blocked off. The box they shared with the Willoughbys, big in the candy

MADRONA ISLAND   23

business, faded into oblivion as the, to Lee, incomprehensible opera unfolded below them. The brilliant footlights gave way in her mind to a memory of glittering hotel foyer chandeliers, the stage given over to a re-enactment of the most wonderful—and most traumatic—time in her life.

Instead of the portly tenor at centre stage, she saw Kelsey's lean, almost slender figure, his eyes lit by an ineradicable flame in their black depths as he bent to whisper into the ear of the slight girl by his side. A girl whose red-gold hair surrounded her face in an untamed mass, whose eyes and mouth betrayed her vulnerability to the wonders of being in love for the first time. The high school boys she had dated faded into the oblivion they deserved when compared to Kelsey's experienced charm. He had known exactly what he was doing when he whispered at her ear that night,

'I have some champagne in my room, will you share it with me?'

The proverbial wolf's age-old tactic for the seduction of the young and innocent! And Lee had fallen for it, hook, line and sinker. Later, devoid of the madness that had seized her senses, she had wondered ashamedly at her own response to his skilled love-making. The champagne bubbles in her blood had no doubt played a part in her seduction, but she could never blame what followed on the effects of the champagne alone.

Her eyes closed, shutting out the discordant music wafting up from the stage. In a silent oasis of her own making, she let herself conjure up that evening in Kelsey's hotel room in living, vivid colour.

'You're so beautiful,' Kelsey had murmured into the silken tumble of her hair, 'so beautiful and—so innocent.' He pulled abruptly away from her on the uncomfortable hotel couch, his black eyes above hungrily prominent cheekbones seeming haunted suddenly. 'I think you'd better go, Lee,' he said abruptly. 'There are things you don't know about me, things that would make you hate me if you knew.'

'Nothing about you could ever make me hate you,' Lee had told him, a husky catch in her voice as she reached for him again. 'I—love you, Kelsey, nothing can change that.'

Nothing. Certainly not the overwhelming effect on her physical senses when he hesitated for only a moment before taking her at her word, the softened outline of his lips plundering the tender fullness of hers, the trembling urgency in his hands as they undid the fastenings of her clothing, the warm rush of sensation as those leanly moulded hands caressed her final, breathless nakedness. The transition from couch to bed was hazy in her memory; all she recalled was the delirious sensation of his hard male flesh against her corresponding softness, the sudden flowering of a womanhood that gladly, joyfully, submitted to the male in him. Pain was transitory when his possession became complete, a storm before the calm that enveloped her when at last he slept by her side, a possessive arm thrown across her.

Fighting off the lethargy that had pervaded her

own limbs, she dreamed lazily of the life ahead of them. Mornings when he would awake to the breakfast she had prepared for him with loving hands, evenings when he would confide the stresses of his day, nights when they would forget the world and concentrate solely on each other. Marriage in all its aspects. . . .

The harsh voice of Dorothy, his sister-in-law, echoed as clearly in her mind as it had that morning when she had awakened to find Kelsey gone from the bed, Dorothy standing mockingly over her.

'I hate to disturb your dreams, but isn't it time you left?' the older woman had said forcefully, her eyes contemptuous as they went over Lee's naked shoulders, which gave more than an ample hint of the nakedness underneath. 'His one-night stands are usually gone before morning.'

'I d-don't know what you mean,' Lee blinked dazedly, pulling the gold-coloured sheet up to chin level. 'Who are you anyway?'

'I'm his brother's wife,' Dorothy returned shortly, her mud-coloured eyes flat in her sallow face as they encountered the confident serenity in Lee's. 'The maids are waiting to clean the room,' she added sharply, 'so please vacate it as soon as possible.'

Lee had gathered the remnants of her dignity around her, facing up to the virago who glared down at her. 'You don't understand. Kelsey and I are—are going to be——' The word 'married' stuck in her throat, although she had no doubt that Kelsey wanted just that after their closeness of the night before.

'Married?' Dorothy laughed coarsely. 'If I had a dollar for every girl who'd hoped for that, I'd be a rich woman! Don't you know that Kelsey's already married?'

Already married . . . the words seemed to echo just as clearly now as they had seven years ago. At first Lee had doubted the word of the sister-in-law who might possibly have had her own axe to grind, but nothing had been able to eradicate the telephone conversation later that day.

'Hi,' he said with the husky intimacy she would have expected under normal circumstances, even though the call was taken in the busy confines of her office as secretary to Fletcher Whitney. 'Why don't you plan on putting on some glad rags and doing the town with me tonight? It's my last in San Francisco for a while.'

Unable to stop the words, Lee asked in a high unnatural voice, 'Are you sure your wife will be able to spare you next time?'

The heavy silence at the other end of the line could have indicated anything. But any hopes Lee might have cherished about his brother's wife lying for some obscure reason of her own were swept away when Kelsey said tightly at last, 'Who told you I'm married?'

'Is that important?' Lee had returned coolly through the hurt that made every nerve end scream in protest. 'The facts are that I didn't know, and that now I do I have no wish to be just another of your casual out-of-town girl-friends!'

'It's not like that, Lee, please listen to me.' How

many others had Kelsey used that dramatically lowered tone with? Lee wondered sourly. 'Let me at least see you, to explain. . . .'

'I think I get the picture without explanations,' Lee cut in curtly. 'Just stay away from me in future, Kelsey. Somewhere along the line I picked up the old-fashioned idea that marriage between two people is—sacred. If I'd known about your marriage,' she choked, 'I certainly wouldn't have—have stayed with you last night.'

Just like that it had been over. If Kelsey had made further trips to San Francisco, she hadn't heard of them. Hadn't wanted to hear of them when the indisputable evidence of her pregnancy made itself obvious in the weeks that followed.

Only Fletcher had known the true circumstances before his offer of marriage. Dear, sweet Fletcher who had had no qualms—at least none she knew about—in facing the ridicule of San Francisco society by taking to wife his young secretary. Not even Lee could gauge the effect of taunting jibes his friends of years had levelled at him, most of them recalling the patrician acceptability of his first wife. It was only in the past couple of years, since Lee had made it obvious that she was interested in no other man, had they come to accept her as one of themselves. Grudgingly, they admired her ability to not only carry on the Whitney Company but to increase its holdings until it was a powerful force to be reckoned with in the corporate world. Her glacial competence inspired no warmth of feeling, but respect for her money-making abilities was unstinting.

Feeling removed from her surroundings, Lee permitted Maitland to lead her from the Opera House, her murmured agreement on comments regarding the performance from the multitude of acquaintances they met coinciding with the opinion of whoever spoke to her. Some had liked it, some had despised. She herself had no opinion. She had seen and heard little of it.

'The Willoughbys are expecting us at their supper party at the Palladium,' Maitland said expansively as they waited for the car to be brought round.

'I'd rather go directly home,' Lee told him with an unusual dash of independence.

'Home?' His fleshy face folded into creases of incomprehension. 'But important people are going to be there, Lee,' he reminded her, uncertain of her in this mood. 'People who could be influential in the future.'

'Then you go,' she returned without rancour. 'I can take a cab home.'

Maitland was as horrified as if she had suggested climbing the spans of the Golden Gate bridge. 'Certainly not! I brought you, and I'll take you home.'

Disgruntled, almost pouting, he directed the chauffeur homeward, parting at the door with such alacrity that Lee suspected he would put in an appearance at the Willoughby party notwithstanding her own absence. Whatever else might be said of him, Maitland's business eye never slept. In all honesty, Lee admitted as she let herself into the Whitney mansion, Maitland was the kingpin in the elaborate fabric of a society which was woven intricately with the strands of sociability and commerce. Much of the business that had come the way of Whitney Enterprises had been due in large part to his acceptance in the social hierarchy of old established families.

As such, he was an invaluable asset of Whitney Enterprises. Whether that, combined with his not unattractive physical attributes, was enough to fill Lee's previously single-orientated life was something that remained to be seen.

CHAPTER TWO

THE Gulf Islands, lying between Vancouver Island and the mainland of British Columbia, passed in leisurely fashion under them as the private Lear jet winged its way from Seattle. Jewelled blue sea lapped possessively the small atolls, oases of green amid the cobalt blue. Trees rushed in a dark green slash to meet the foaming breakers separating in a white froth on the rocky foreshores, making the occasional houses, perched high for panoramic water views, seem isolated in the wildness of their surroundings.

Lee glanced downward with detachment at first, then leaned sideways with sharper interest. What kind of people inhabited the rocky shores of these islands? The retired, people who had fled from the hustle of North America's cities? Young people, disillusioned by those same city values? Small vegetable plots, incongruously bounded by high wired fencing, prompted her query to the pilot of the Roberts craft.

'Deer are prolific on some of the islands,' he explained, his open face cheerful. 'They'll eat every green sprout in sight, given half a chance.'

Lesser islands, sparsely inhabited, flashed under the jet's body as it lowered for landing. One of them had to be Madrona Island, the Roberts' property, but Lee forbore questioning the pilot as to her final destination. She would know soon enough.

An icy calm descended on her as the plane banked in preparation for landing. Would Kelsey be waiting there on the runway? She hoped not. The *dénouement* she had in mind was destined to take place in a private spot, with no one but Kelsey and herself present. Unless—her eyes narrowed behind dark glasses—his wife was a witness to the confrontation. That would be icing on the cake.

Her fears were unfounded, however. There was no sign of Kelsey's distinctive figure in the vicinity when Lee stepped from the jet and found herself enveloped in the same care she had known in Seattle on alighting from the regular airline flight. She had been whisked then to the Lear jet, just as now she was taken on a short car ride to the jetty where a sleek blue and white cabin cruiser awaited her.

Madrona Island, pointed out to her by the young boatman, lay within view of the wharf, its seeming closeness deceptive as the cruiser went inexorably towards it. Like the other islands in the Gulf, Madrona sported a healthy growth of trees, their bending trunks undulating gracefully out over the leeside waters caressing the island. As she approached nearer, Lee's interest was caught by the bright red bark and leathery dark green leaves of the trees, as well as their twisted, somewhat tortuous growth rising from the barren-looking rocks.

Seeing her interest, the young jeans-clad man steering the cruiser proffered the information that the trees were arbutus, native to the rocky coastal shorelines.

'Arbutus—madrona,' he shrugged, 'they mean the same.'

'So that's where the island gets its name,' Lee stated obviously, her mind only partially absorbed in the distinctive landscape. Foolishly, she had made no plans as to how she would make her dignified withdrawal from the island. If she had thought about it at all, it was only to assume that there would be transport at her command. Now, as the young seaman piloted the neat craft into a natural harbour carved sideways into the island, she wondered if his base was there or on the mainland they had just left.

That thought faded abruptly from her mind when an impressive brown lodge-type structure hove into view. Set back on a hilly rise, the rustic pillared house commanded the narrow inlet while being tucked out of sight of passing shipping. Terraced gardens, brilliant with summer blooming flowers, sloped down to smooth green lawns which seemed to have been sliced from the thick bush and trees on either side.

Belated apprehension clutched at Lee's throat as she looked up from watching the expert handling of the cruiser as it nudged against the sturdy but weathered jetty extending out from a small curve of sand beach. A movement close to the house had caught her eye. Kelsey? An irrepressible surge of relief washed over her when she discerned the hurrying figure of a middle-aged woman dressed in a bright floral print. Immediately she berated herself. She had come here to confront Kelsey, hadn't she? Whether it was now or later was immaterial.

That it would be later was obvious from the creases worrying the older woman's brow, a frown that seemed to deepen as Lee stepped with the boatman's

help on to the pier. Her light brown eyes widened in
stunned surprise when they went over Lee's graceful
figure elegantly clad in white skirt suit and blue
patterned blouse that frothed in soft folds at her
neck.

'We—we were expecting a Mrs Whitney,' she
forced out breathlessly. 'Was she not able to come
herself?'

'I'm Mrs Whitney,' Lee returned coolly, and
turned to the openly staring young man who, she saw
now with distaste, sported bare brown feet. 'My luggage?' she reminded him pointedly, and he immediately leapt back into the boat and hoisted her
hide suitcases, two of them, on to the jetty.

'Bring them up to the house, will you, Geoff?' the
woman asked, standing back to allow Lee to precede
her along the wooden pier. 'Mr Kelsey was really
upset that he had to stay here and take a long-dist-
ance telephone call,' she apologised. 'He meant to
come over and meet the plane, of course.'

'Of course,' Lee returned with a hint of irony that
wasn't lost on the older woman who panted by her
side, hurrying to keep up with Lee's businesslike
stride. 'Has the other guest arrived?'

'Other——?' Obviously mystified, the woman
blinked up into Lee's level gaze. 'Mr Kelsey must
have forgotten to tell me,' she clucked then, shaking
her head. 'It wouldn't be the first time either, but it
makes no matter. We always have a bed or two made
up.' Indicating a curve of flat rock steps leading up to
an old brick terrace fronting the house, she added,
'We can go in this way.'

Fulsome hanging baskets with their cascades of trailing lobelia, orange-red geraniums, downcurving nepeta positioned between the brown supports marked her passage, but Lee was oblivious to them. Somewhere within these walls was the man she had come over a thousand miles to vent her spleen on. The very thought had the power to dry up the moist areas of her mouth, to parch her throat.

'I'm Freda Gilbert, by the way,' the short woman divulged as she slid aside a long glass door leading into a huge room which obviously served as both hall and living room. Comfortable-looking sofas and chairs in restful green floral cotton were placed to take advantage of the garden and ocean views; black leather settees faced each other more soberly at either side of a massive natural rock fireplace that soared as high as the galleried upper floor.

Followed by the barefoot Geoff, Lee crossed between the furnishings to the staircase tucked away at the far side of the hall.

'That's Mr Kelsey's study,' Freda indicated a solid door leading off a spacious landing halfway up the broad and shallow red-carpeted stairs, 'but he'll no doubt want to show you the house himself later on.' Leading the way up the last short flight of stairs, she chattered on, 'I'll show you to your room now, and have tea ready for you on the terrace in half an hour, will that be all right?'

Lee murmured something, she didn't know what. She was too conscious that only the thickness of that door separated her from the man she hated. The force of her feelings made her dizzy for a moment so that she stumbled near the top step and had to clutch the wide, elaborately carved banister. The housekeeper, walking ahead, noticed nothing, and from Geoff's heavy breathing behind her his attention was concentrated solely on toting the heavy suitcases.

The carved oak rail continued along a broad passage leading to the bedrooms, and Lee found herself looking directly down on the living room they had just left. How much of the ambience in this house was due to Kelsey's taste? Ancient armoires lined the broad carpeted passage on her left, and even the smell of the house spoke of subdued good taste. His wife's, or perhaps his brother's wife's, or a combination of both?

Freda branched right off the gallery and threw open a door to what was virtually a private suite. The room they entered first was furnished as a bedroom in a tasteful blending of colour from shell pink to deepest scarlet with relieving touches of white.

'The sitting room is through here,' Freda continued as Lee dropped her vanity case on the white dressing table before following the older woman, 'and you have a beautiful view of the islands and water.'

The room was lovely, a series of narrow latticed windows giving on to the view of trees and azure water, heat-hazed islands mirage-like in the distance. Leaf-patterned beige cretonne covered the long window seat and the easy chairs scattered around the room, and there was even a chaise-longue placed to take advantage of the restful views.

'It's very nice,' Lee approved coolly, obviously disappointing the housekeeper with her lukewarm praise. Turning back into the bedroom, Lee put the question that had been at the back of her mind since this meeting had first been arranged. 'Is—Mrs Roberts here at the moment?'

'Oh, no!' Freda seemed almost shocked. 'She's with Mr Phil in Seattle. They do come here sometimes,' she elaborated, her fingers busily investigating the dressing table top for signs of dust, 'but Mr Phil doesn't care too much for the island.'

'I meant Mrs Kelsey Roberts,' Lee explained, feigning casualness as she sprang open the locks on the cases Geoff had laid dutifully on the luggage holder at the foot of the double bed. 'Is she here?'

Freda stared at her in shock. 'Oh, no, Mrs Whitney. Mr Kelsey's wife died last year in a car crash, and he hasn't married again. Poor man, it was very sad.'

Lee swung round to face the headshaking housekeeper. 'What happened?' Her own head had an insane desire to shake with Freda's.

'Well,' the old-time servant hesitated, in two minds whether to gossip about her employer's business, 'Mr Kelsey was driving at the time. They had been to a party and it had been raining, and Mr Kelsey couldn't control the car when it swerved off the road. Mrs Susan was—killed outright, and he was unconscious for days after, couldn't remember a thing. Even now. . . .' she shook her head commiseratingly again.

'Even now—what?' Lee asked sharply.

'His memory is very patchy,' Freda explained softly. 'He recalls some things, but not others. It was his head that was struck, you see.' She visibly shook herself and gave Lee a bright smile. 'Tea will be on the terrace in half an hour, Mrs Whitney. Straight through the living room and to your left.'

Thanking her absently, Lee stood thoughtfully where she was for several moments after the house-keeper had gone, then crossed the scarlet broadloom to stare out of the window to where another side of the island was revealed. A narrower lawn close to the house gave way to a dense forest area which in turn yielded to a wide expanse of ocean, a westering sun slanting its yellow glow over waters as glassy calm as a millpond. Peaceful now, but what would it be like when winter whipped up the grey sea to white-topped fury, when sunless days made the forest even more impenetrable than it now was?

Fanciful thought, designed to keep away the questions crowding in her mind. It was as if a bomb had shattered the pattern her life had assumed in the past few years. Groping, Lee sought to find the motivating hatred that had guided her actions since that night in Kelsey's hotel room. How sure she had been that night that Kelsey loved her, that the intimacy she had permitted would lead inevitably to marriage.

Permitted! Angrily she swept aside the floor-length side curtain and pinned it back with her hand clenched on the window frame. She had been no match for Kelsey's expertise in matters of love. The expert caress of his hands, mouth, body, had reduced resistance to the unfamiliarity of passion, melting her bones and flaming her veins with his urgency. Later, knowing how he had used her, her own responses had been a source of horror and shame, a shame that had firmed to hatred on discovering that she was to bear Kelsey's child.

Could it make any difference now that the woman he had been married to was dead? That Kelsey himself had been injured in that same accident, his memory affected by it? Lee's breath held in suspension for an agonising moment. Was it possible—could it be possible that he remembered nothing of what had transpired between them years ago? *That he didn't remember her?*

Something—a movement, perhaps, or her acutely raised senses—made her turn from the window. The door had been pushed wide, and framed there was the tall, well-knit figure of a man. Kelsey.

Lee felt the blood drain from her face, the moment of *dénouement* she had lived for lost in the deep surge of discomposure that swept through her and left her body raglike, her legs seeming rooted in insubstantial cotton. Nevertheless, her slow-moving gaze took in the high planed contours of his face, the faint blue shadow on determined jaw, the thinly contoured lips parted slightly to reveal a narrow glimpse of white teeth. The black hair was still thick and black, the body broadened and obviously muscular in white knit shirt and the casual blue of faded jeans.

He was the same, yet different in a way she knew subconsciously was irreversible. There was a hardness to his jaw that had not been there before, a maturity in his bearing, a bitter cast to the almost black eyes which now stared at her with no hint of surprise. Had he known her identity all along? Had she registered so little on his consciousness that he found no connection between the elegantly groomed woman he saw now and the naïve girl who had spent a night with him in his hotel room seven years before? She had changed in those years from a starry-eyed girl in a bargain basement cotton dress to a poised woman in charge of herself and her life. Her hair, elegantly coiled in the grecian style she had become accustomed to, was far removed from the long fall of baby-fine light gold that he had woven through his fingers, telling her a woman's hair was truly her crowning glory, a proclamation of her femininity. She had been only one of many indulgences he allowed himself on his frequent business travels, according to his brother's wife, Dorothy.

Or could the mind-shattering possibility be true, that he genuinely didn't remember her from seven years ago, the car accident claiming part of his memory processes?

'Mrs Whitney, I presume.' The softly spoken words were said more as a statement than a question, and Lee decided to play the scene by ear, going along with Kelsey's seeming acceptance of herself at face value.

'Yes,' she returned evenly, 'and you are Mr Roberts?'

His dark head made a bare inclination. 'Is everything to your satisfaction?' His eyes went cursorily round the eminently comfortable suite, then came back to rest on her impersonally.

'Perfectly.' Lee made a gesture towards the windows. 'The views are wonderful. It's a—beautiful place.' She clasped her hands in front of her to conceal their uncertain trembling, and clenched the even

whiteness of her teeth in an effort to control the jang-
ling awareness of her nerve ends.

'I like it.' Kelsey pushed himself away from the
doorframe and indicated the passage with one dark-
skinned hand. 'Are you ready to come downstairs and
have what Freda calls afternoon tea? The house isn't
all that big, but some people have trouble finding
their way down at first.'

'I—yes, thank you.' Lee, although she hadn't done
so much as wash her hands in the luxuriously appointed suite, went past Kelsey into the corridor
beyond and walked beside him with thumping heart
across the gallery passage and down the broad red-
carpeted stairs.

'I'm sorry I couldn't make it to the plane to meet
you,' he apologised, his fingers lightly guiding on her
white-suited elbow. 'A crisis came up and I had to
deal with it personally.'

His hand tightened on her elbow when she stumbled
on reaching the small landing outside his study. But it
wasn't the thickness of carpet under her slenderly
heeled shoes that made her falter in her step, it was a
thought which had occurred to her as they descended
from the upper floor. If Kelsey hadn't recognised
her—and it seemed obvious he hadn't—the reason
for her journey here was no longer valid. Leading
him and the shipping line principal on to believe she
was seriously interested in the deal before dropping
the idea cold would only be effective if Kelsey was
aware of her reasons for doing it. Sweetness would
change to bitterness in a revenge that meant nothing
to him. Her brow wrinkled in thought, she accom-

panied Kelsey through the living room area and stepped by him on to the broad brick terrace.

The housekeeper, Freda, had just finished unloading the last of the afternoon snack when they walked together across the uneven bricks to where, half hidden by the graceful fronds of white-flowered vining plant, a green checked table groaned under plates of sandwiches, small individual iced cakes, and a heavy silver tray with matching accoutrements for the serving of tea.

'Thanks, Freda,' said Kelsey, a note of wry humour in his quietly pitched voice as he held an elaborately scrolled white garden chair for Lee and seated her at the table. 'I think this should see us through until dinner.'

'If you need anything more, Mr Kelsey,' Freda returned comfortably, 'you know where I am.' She disappeared through another sliding door directly off the patio, and Lee saw the reflected dining room furniture through the uncurtained windows.

'She's English, isn't she?' she asked for want of something better to say, and Kelsey smiled briefly, waving his hand across the laden table.

'What else? Cucumber sandwiches, egg and cress sandwiches, what she calls fairy cakes, and tea strong enough to tar a road! But I must say,' he swivelled the tray round so that Lee had only to lift a hand to reach the high arched handle of the silver teapot, 'I'm getting used to this graceful English habit late in the afternoon. Will you be mother?'

Startled, Lee stared at him speechlessly. All she had heard was 'mother,' a word that was altogether too close to home where Kelsey was concerned. But for a trick of fate, she would indeed be mother to a six-year-old child, fathered by the man opposite.

'It's an English expression,' Kelsey explained, puzzled. 'They say that——'

'I know,' Lee hurried to pick up the elaborate pot and pour the dark brown liquid in the rose-patterned teacups laid ready. 'I like tea, and I like it strong, as the English do.' Handing him his cup, she then offered milk and sugar, both of which he refused. 'What's happened to the principal you spoke about?' she went on briskly, selecting a lump of sugar with the tongs provided and colouring her own tea with milk. 'I understood he was to be here too.'

'That was the arrangement, but unfortunately he's been detained for a few days—business, which I'm sure you'll understand.'

An overwhelming surge of uncertainty tightened Lee's fingers on the shapely handle of her cup. Had all her instincts been wrong in telling her that Kelsey had no knowledge of her real identity, that the deal with this faceless, nameless principal had been a fake from the start?

'Who—who is he, this principal? What's his name?'

'Harry Vendisi,' Kelsey returned smoothly, helping himself to one of the crustless sandwiches and disposing of its three-cornered smallness in two bites. When Lee looked blank, he reached for another and smiled wryly. 'You've never heard of him? That's not surprising. He keeps a pretty low profile in his business affairs, they're quite varied.'

Vendisi? Varied business affairs? Lee's brows knotted in thought momentarily, then visibly relaxed. It was ridiculous to suppose that, because a man possessed an Italian name and had varied business interests, he was connected with other than totally legitimate commerce. Kelsey's low chuckle brought her eyes up to meet the wicked gleam in his.

'You're right,' he said. 'Harry's connected to the underworld, though I'm not sure how completely. All I know is that he's giving up the shipping part of the operation, and it's too good an opportunity to pass up.'

'You mean he's——?' Lee's voice faded away in indignation, but in another moment she had regained her self-possession and gazed frostily across the crowded table into Kelsey's amused eyes. 'I'm not accustomed to doing business with—with members of the underworld, Mr Roberts.'

Unperturbed, Kelsey disposed of the sandwich and stretched out a hand to his cup. 'Why not? His shipping business is entirely legitimate, cleaner than most because it's been his cover for years.'

'Why is he getting rid of it now?' Lee asked suspiciously. 'Why doesn't he need a cover any more?'

'Because he's found other interests that present less of a hassle to him than running the shipping line,' Kelsey answered blandly, draining his cup and holding it out to Lee for a refill. 'Don't worry, Mrs Whitney,' he mocked, 'you won't be held accountable for Harry's past sins. The deal I told you about is entirely above board, no strings attached.'

Lee poured tea into his cup and absently added to

her own. This was an entirely new situation for her, and she was lost. In the labyrinthine depths of the business world, was it ethically possible to condemn the activities of a man like Harry Vendisi on the one hand, while on the other calmly to arrange to take over a part of his business which was legitimate?

Seeing her hesitation, Kelsey offered a noncommittal solution. 'Wait until you meet him before making up your mind. As I've said, it's a once-in-a-lifetime opportunity that could mean a lot to both of us.'

Both of us! As if they were joined in close friendship, as if. . . .

'I'm not sure I want to wait here on Mr Vendisi's pleasure,' said Lee, glancing disparagingly over the terraced gardens and lawns stretching down to the cove. 'It's not exactly a hive of industry, is it?'

'No,' he admitted without rancour, his eyes darkly brilliant as they rested on the delicate paleness of her skin. 'But maybe a holiday in the sun would do you good. You can swim down there,' he nodded towards the bay, 'or in the pool at the other side of the house. We have a tennis court, badminton, croquet outdoors, table tennis, billiards, and any number of indoor occupations. When did you last take a vacation?' he ended abruptly.

'Vacation?' Lee stared at him nonplussed. 'I— don't have time to waste in the way you're suggesting, Mr Roberts. Whitney Enterprises would soon go on the downslide if its President elected to follow the pursuits you mention.'

'Rubbish!' he said forcefully, his lean jaw clenching in a way she remembered too well. 'Getting away from it for a while, spacing yourself, lets you come back to it with fresh ideas and the energy to put them into practice.'

'I've managed quite well without indulging in useless pursuits,' Lee retorted with stony irony. 'Whitney Enterprises has prospered to the tune of quadrupling its interests during the time I've been its President. I assure you our stockholders have no qualms about my lack of expertise on the tennis courts!'

Kelsey stared at her with disconcerting frankness for a long moment. 'You're very young to be kingpin in an organisation like Whitney's,' he said speculatively at last. 'Your husband was a lot older than you, wasn't he?'

It was on the tip of Lee's tongue to retort that he should know what Fletcher's age had been at the time of their marriage, but she bit it back. If he really remembered nothing of herself, it was even less likely that he remembered his own impecunious advances to Fletcher.

'What does that have to do with anything?' she parried instead, stretching out a cool hand to take up one of the cucumber sandwiches and nibbling on it while conscious of Kelsey's calculating appraisal.

'What made you marry a man so much older than yourself?'

Lee choked delicately on the bread she had just bitten into. 'For his money, what else?' she mocked on her recovery. 'I don't suppose you'd believe, any more than his friends and associates believed at the time, that I loved Fletcher.' She took a soothing mouthful of tea before meeting his brooding gaze again.

'And did you? Love him?'

'Isn't that a very personal question, Mr Roberts? But yes, since you ask, I loved Fletcher very much. He died five years ago, but I still miss him.' She paused deliberately. 'As I'm sure you miss your wife.'

If her motive had been to disconcert him, she was amply rewarded in the brief flare of pain that filled his dark eyes and spilled over, unaccountably, into her own heart.

'I see Freda's been filling you in on my personal history too,' he said quietly, pushing back his chair with a scrape across the bricks and standing beside her. 'Would you like to see over the house before going up to your room? I imagine you're tired after travelling for a good part of the day.'

'I am a little,' Lee admitted, standing, 'but yes, I would like to see the house. What particular style is it?' she asked constrictedly as they moved to the tall glass doors Freda had used.

'No particular style as far as I know,' Kelsey answered in the same impersonal tone. 'The house was already here when we bought the island a few years ago. A Canadian industrialist acquired it for his retirement and had the house built and the gardens laid out, but his wife died before they moved here, so he never did live on the island.'

'Were the furnishings his?' she enquired coolly, looking round the spacious dining room they had entered, noting the heavy antiquity of rectangular table and ladderbacked chairs, the solid aged wood of the sideboards and server tables. Even to her unpractised eye they spelt taste and vast expense.

'No. I furnished the place myself.'

His abrupt answer gave her food for thought, thoughts that followed her into the living room with its massive fireplace and through to a small sitting room which also faced out to the garden and ocean views. Did Kelsey really command this much decorative taste? Although the various rooms were furnished with pieces from differing eras, there was a superb blending of the whole. In this small sitting room, for instance, comfortable tub chairs in bright prints contrasted with elegantly contoured provincial tables and chairs without disharmony. A woman's room, this was, with its blend of formal and country-style ease.

'Your wife must have had a hand in this room,' she said impulsively, uncaring or perhaps needling him into the same kind of pained display he had shown earlier on mention of his wife.

'No,' he said abruptly, moving back towards the white painted door. 'She never visited the island. Susan was the kind who needed people around her at all times.'

Inexplicable pleasure rippled through Lee, but there was no time then to analyse the feeling as Kelsey went with long strides through the rest of the house. The kitchen, where Freda was preparing the evening meal, was bypassed. It was only when, having viewed the intimately monastic study where Kelsey conducted his business and a sampling of the

bedrooms on the upper floor, none of them as elaborately furnished as her own suite of rooms, that she had
time to think of her changed situation.

Stretched on the chaise-longue in the sitting room
off her bedroom, clad lightly in the azure blue of
the robe she had substituted for the white travel suit,
she stared out at the darkening view and made an
effort to organise her thoughts into familiar pat-
terns.

But obstinately they refused to be marshalled. The
hatred she had nourished for so long seemed lost in a
limbo of cotton candy clouds. The searing flame of
her revengeful dream had made no allowance for her
own reactions on seeing, being with, Kelsey again.
She had been unprepared for the effect his physical
presence would have on her, the hard male appeal of
his muscularly fit body. The arms that had held her
in passion were the same she had seen that afternoon,
sinewy and with a generous covering of blackly virile
hairs. His mouth, though narrower in line, was still
the mouth that had had the power to make her
forget, for that one night, a morality she had
absorbed through her pores from earliest childhood.

The deep hatred that had sustained her for years
had disappeared into some kind of limbo, and she was
left without the prop that had made her drive to the
top singleminded. What Kelsey had done to her all
those years ago was unforgivable. But how did a
person go about extracting revenge on a man who
didn't even remember her existence? The stark realisation hit Lee that she would have to go through with
this masquerade, to pretend an interest she didn't feel

in the proposition she had ostensibly come here to negotiate.

She watched the sky as it streaked gold and flame across the horizon, outlining the pines in stark relief against its colourful background. With a speed which would have surprised her, Lee fell into a deep, troubled sleep.

CHAPTER THREE

LEE found her way without trouble to the lower floor, her steps smaller than usual because of the confining design of her dress.

Awakened to startled surprise when Freda clicked on the soft pink glow of table lamps in the sitting room of the suite, she had rushed to shower and dress in the time the housekeeper had allotted before dinner. At some time, perhaps while she and Kelsey had been taking tea on the terrace, Lee's clothes had been taken from the suitcases and hung in the spacious closets and laid out in the capacious drawers under and surrounding them.

The choice of her close-fitting black dress had been made hurriedly, its just-below-knee length seeming a fitting style to wear for the casual informality of the house. Even if Kelsey wore evening clothes, the dress would still be suitable. Diamonds at her throat and ears completed her ensemble, and she felt reasonably confident as she entered the huge living room and saw Kelsey, his back to her, standing motionless before the fireplace. The dark suit he wore, with its rim of white collar beneath his black hair, was as tastefully chosen as her own for dinner in a country house.

He seemed unaware of her presence, so Lee said

huskily, 'Am I late? I'm afraid I fell asleep, and Freda had to wake me. Travelling is more tiring than I thought it would be.'

Kelsey swung round as she started to speak, his surprise giving way to a long male appraisal of her figure as she stood at the entrance to the living room. An inner quiver, one she hoped would not surface, shivered over Lee when his black eyes went with leisurely appreciation over the creamy exposure of her shoulders to the faint glimpse of rounded breasts above a severely narrowed waistline to hips flaring in their confinement under the restrictive contours of her dress. His acute gaze took in the slender length of her calves before returning slowly to her carefully made up face.

'You're not late,' he said belatedly, lifting his arm to indicate that she should join him before the glistening rock of the fireplace. 'What will you have to drink?'

'I usually have a Martini before dinner,' Lee forced her reluctant feet towards the sofa nearest the entrance, 'but a dry sherry would do.' She sat at one end of the sofa, her arm stretched along its black leather.

'Strange,' Kelsey mused, moving to the shelved bar to one side of the fireplace area, 'I'd have sworn you were a sweet sherry girl.'

Lee's muscles tensed. Her unschooled taste at eighteen *had* run on sweet lines. Sweet sherry, sweet desserts, sweet first love. . . .

'Anything dry will do,' she told him, her body taut under the expensive model dress she wore.

Accepting the pale glass of exquisitely cut crystal Kelsey handed her, she tasted its contents of sharp dryness without change of expression. 'That's fine, thank you.'

Instead of resuming his place in front of the fireplace, Kelsey sat easily in the far corner of the sofa, his arm resting on its leather back while he looked appraisingly at her.

'You intrigue me,' he said, smiling, his eyes flickering from hers down to the neat conformation of her breasts under the barely concealing bodice of her dress. 'You married a man so much older than yourself, and since his death you've proved yourself a more astute businessman than he ever was. I've met people who knew him, and they say he was a steady plodder who would never have taken Whitney Enterprises to the heights you have. You have a finger in just about every pie known to the corporate world, yet you sit there without any life or animation in you. Haven't you ever thought of marrying again?'

'Have you?' she countered, stung.

'Oh, yes,' he said softly, the liquid darkness of his eyes a caress when they met and held the icy blue of hers. 'I'm not cut out for the single life.'

'And who's the lucky lady to be?' Lee mocked, dropping her own gaze to the glass she held lightly in her hand. The stabbing thrust in her chest was far removed from jealousy; what ground into her soul was the thought that Kelsey felt himself free to live and love with a woman of his choice, while he had left her a shell devoid of passion.

'I'm not sure yet.'

Lee's hand trembled slightly as she lifted the glass to her lips. 'You have a wide area to choose from, no doubt,' she said drily, slanting contempt in the look she gave him.

'Not really, if what they say is true that there's an ideal mate if you search long enough.' His voice held the lazy drawl it had when he was amused and Lee retorted crushingly,

'You can't really believe that sentimental claptrap! It's certainly not the kind of thinking that takes people to the top in the business world—none that I concern myself with, anyway.'

Her subtle hint that their own business dealings depended on her powerful sway registered as a faint gleam in Kelsey's eye as he rose lithely and took her diminished glass from her hand.

'Let me get you a refill,' he said easily, walking with his lithe stride to the drinks cabinet. Almost against her will, Lee watched him, noting the strong grace of his well-kept hands, the subdued ripple of muscle as he reached for bottles. Something about her own reluctant interest irritated her when the thought came to her that she hadn't been wrong. Kelsey Roberts would have his choice from any of the many women who must come within his orbit. Hadn't she capitulated without a struggle even when he had been less broadly mature and confident?

He turned from the bar while her eyes were still on him, and a faint tinge of colour put pink into her cheeks. What had he read into that look of hers? That she was as fallible as the next woman? For a moment, while she took the glass from him and felt his fingers brush hers casually, she wished that he *would* treat her in the same way as the other attractive women he knew. The pleasure of going along with it before spurning him decisively would be like nectar in her revengeful veins. But it would be a dangerous game to play, she realised, with a man like Kelsey. His experience far outmatched her own, and she never went into any deal without the stakes being even or weighed in her favour.

'You didn't answer my question,' he said now from the fireplace, where he had taken up his stance.

'What question was that?'

'If you're thinking of marrying again.'

Her brows drew together in an irritated frown. 'I didn't come here to talk about my personal life, Mr Roberts, which is none of your business. It can't possibly interest you whether I intend marrying again or not.'

'Maybe not, under normal circumstances,' he conceded, unruffled. 'But we're going to be in each other's company almost exclusively for the next two weeks, and we can't talk business all the time.' He looked at her over the rim of his glass. 'I find it hard to think about business at all when I'm in the company of a beautiful woman.'

Lee gave him a sarcastic glance. 'Thank you for the compliment,' she said drily, 'but if that's so, you should have asked Maitland Frasier, my right-hand man, to come in my place.'

Kelsey looked at her thoughtfully as if he had heard a significance she had not intended in her words. 'Maitland Frasier . . . San Francisco's blue-eyed boy? I heard while I was down there that he's your main squire around town. Is he to be Number Two?'

Lee stared at him frigidly without answering, and felt an overwhelming sense of relief when Freda put in an appearance from the back area of the house.

'I've laid the table in the small sitting room, Mr Kelsey,' she announced breathlessly, 'as there's only the two of you.'

'That's fine, Freda, thanks. Is dinner ready now?'

At her nod, he finished the remainder of his drink and set his glass down on the square coffee table before coming to hold out a politely helping hand to Lee. A quiver shot like quicksilver up her arm when his warm grasp enveloped her small-boned hand, and she instinctively jerked it away when she was on her feet. A slight tightening of his mouth was the only sign Kelsey gave that he had noticed the gesture and, undeterred, his hand slid under her elbow as they walked towards the room they were to dine in.

'Don't you think we could dispense with the Mr Roberts and Mrs Whitney thing?' he suggested as he seated her at the round intimacy of the small table placed against the window. Darkness had fallen outside, but Lee saw the comforting twinkle of lights from a distant island. 'You know what my name is, but all I've heard you called is Mrs Fletcher Whitney. You do have a name of your own, I presume?'

Her mouth twisted in derision. 'Did you think my parents had named me for the husband I would marry one day? My name is——' she hesitated. Would mention of her name light any glimmer of memory in his injured mind?

'Don't tell me, let me guess.' He stared at her appraisingly while Freda brought in their appetiser of plump shrimps set on beds of chilled lettuce and highlighted by a tangy red sauce. Kelsey's deep gaze embarrassed her suddenly and she picked up the small-tined fork to start on her portion. 'Helen, that's it,' he said at last, 'beautiful but cold.'

The description inexplicably hurt her and she swallowed hard, almost choking. Like a ghost from the past, the voice that now searched for her name echoed in memory the hot passionate outpouring of that name into her eighteen-year-old ear.

'You couldn't be more wrong.'

His brows lifted in mocking enquiry. 'In what connection? The name, or the coldness?'

'You'd be a better judge of a woman's temperament,' she retorted acidly. 'I've no intention of discussing that with you. My name is Lee,' she ended abruptly, not caring now and almost wishing that he *would* remember. It would cut short this visit which stretched interminably before her.

'L-e-i-g-h, or L-e-e?' he spelled out, seeming to make no connection with either spelling of her name.

'L-e-e,' she confirmed abruptly.

For a few moments he concentrated on the food before him, then his head went to one side consideringly. 'That's a name that could go either way. Cold now, but room for improvement.'

'Can we get off this ridiculous subject?' Lee snapped irritably, spearing the largest shrimp on the dish with a violence that shocked even herself.

'What would you prefer? That I ask you for the

latest profit and loss sheets on the Frantug operation?'

'Since you ask, yes.' Lee directed a frosty gaze across the table. 'I'm here to discuss business, Mr Roberts, not to have my character analysed by an amateur soothsayer!'

Kelsey winced. 'Ouch! All right, Mrs Whitney, we'll talk business.'

And he did, constantly, incessantly, all through the broiled salmon and the lemon soufflé that followed, right to the time Freda served rich black coffee, until even Lee felt she would scream if she heard one more word about the minor intricacies of managing a tugboat operation.

Only partially acknowledging Kelsey's obvious expertise in matters of business, Lee said wearily after drinking deeply of the coffee, 'I have all the necessary information in my briefcase upstairs. Offhand I can't confirm your figures, but perhaps we can have a session in the morning and go over everything then.' Her eyelashes, thinly coated with darkening mascara, seemed extra heavy and needed some effort to keep them up over the dimmed intelligence in her eyes. The wine, she thought, stifling a yawn with her raised hand. Kelsey, between long monologues, had kept her glass well filled. 'If you'll excuse me now, I'll say goodnight. It's been a long day.'

Under other circumstances, Kelsey's dismayed look might have been funny. 'But it's only nine-thirty! I thought we might have a game of pool before calling it a day.'

'I don't—play pool,' Lee said heavily.

'Then it's time you learned,' Kelsey returned forcefully, getting to his feet and pulling her to hers. 'You'll have your first lesson tonight, and by the time you leave here you'll be an expert.'

Incapable of resistance, Lee allowed herself to be half-dragged from the sitting room and along a back passage which led to a flight of stairs into the basement. The lights Kelsey switched on bathed the extensive area in light as bright as day, and revealed a veritable gym of sports equipment. So this is how he keeps fit, Lee conjectured dully, her eyes going from vaulting horse to punching bag, from rowing machine to exercise bicycle. A ping-pong table at one side of the room gave pride of place to the pool table at its centre.

Kelsey, his hand warm round hers, pulled her to the centre and released her while he switched on the shaded overhead lamps. Turning then to a freestanding cue holder, he selected two and handed one to her.

'The idea is,' he explained, 'to hit the white ball in such a way as to——'

'Scatter the coloured ones into the pockets,' she finished for him, her voice indicating the boredom she felt at the prospect of chasing coloured balls around the green baize cloth.

'It's not quite as simple as that,' Kelsey said drily, hoisting his cue and bending with it over the table edge to aim at the clustered balls. The resulting roll in various directions caught her interest fleetingly, but as Kelsey went on with his solitary game she grew more and more bored until at last she stifled a yawn. Seeing it, Kelsey came back round the table and replaced his cue in the holder.

'Come on, let's see you try,' he suggested, coming up behind Lee lifting the lifeless arm that still held the cue. 'Doing is more fun than watching.'

Lee's body stiffened defensively. 'Not for me,' she said crisply. 'I can't see the sense in chasing balls around a table, or round a golf course for that matter.'

'Does everything have to make sense?' His voice was husky, coming from just behind her ear in a close intimacy that numbed her into immobility. 'All work and no play can make Jill a very dull girl.' His free hand came to rest lightly on the curved indentation of her waist, and the crushing realisation came to Lee that he was making an all too obvious pass at her.

'I didn't get to where I am today by being a fun-loving Jill,' she said stonily, the pool cue dropping from her hand as she twisted her body to face him and found herself trapped between him and the table.

'It shows,' Kelsey told her softly, his eyes making a too-close appraisal of her features before his fingers came up to trace lightly the faint lines on her fore-head and beside her eyes, the firm compression of her full lips. Lee stood immobile, feeling nothing as his touch, which she had yearned so for years before, ran smoothly over her skin. 'You're a young and very beautiful woman, there must be hundreds of men who've wanted to tell you that. But you're all sewn up inside, aren't you? Why, Lee? Did somebody hurt you once?'

Lee wanted to laugh hysterically and tell him that, yes, she had been hurt—by him, because in her in-nocence she had believed that he loved her with the same passion that had fired her eighteen-year-old soul. But the numbness she felt in his presence now, as well as the careful schooling of her emotions since that time, made her speechless.

'You have such beautiful hair, why do you scrape it away from your face like that?' Kelsey's fingers reached behind her head and began to remove the confining pins from the red-gold chignon tightly secured above her nape.

'Don't!' She jerked her head sideways, but too late. Her hair fell, cascaded, tumbled round the creamy whiteness of her bare shoulders, and Kelsey drew in a sharp breath.

'Why would you want to hide it?' he breathed almost reverentially, his hand rising again to drift across the golden top and stroke lightly downward until his fingers separated the long strands. 'My God, you're more beautiful than I thought!'

Even if she hadn't been fatally trapped between his body and the table Lee couldn't have done anything to prevent the quick descent of his head, the hard pressure of his mouth on hers. Her body seemed devoid of motion, of feeling, as his arms locked around her and pulled her, unresisting, to the hard length of him.

Her brain registered the muscled contours of the chest her palms rested impersonally against, the quick-ened sound of his breathing, the forceful parting of her lips by his, but the frozen depths of her remained that way . . . frozen.

It seemed hours, or it could have been minutes, until Kelsey realised that his lovemaking, however expert, wasn't reaching her. His mouth still against hers, his hands made a slow progress from her rounded hips to her shoulders and finally pushed her from him. His heart under her palm had a deep, aroused resonance, a pulse that thundered through his chest. His nostrils flared with the breath rushing through them as he stared at her, his eyes twin fires of disbelieving question as they raked hers.

'You really don't care about anything but Whitney Enterprises, do you?' he mocked in a hard voice, dropping his hands from her shoulders and stepping back a pace. 'A woman with corporate ice in her veins.'

Lee, unmoved, lifted the strap of her dress back to her shoulder and stepped round him. 'It's a whole new world in business today, Mr Roberts, or hadn't you heard? Deals are no longer consummated on the executive couch. The only way you'll get Frantug is if you come up with a better deal than any other bidder.'

'To hell with Frantug!' Kelsey's face seemed to have paled beneath the healthy tan he sported. 'All I'm interested in is——'

'Mr Vendisi's property?' Lee asked sweetly, putting space between them as she walked to the stairway. 'We'll have to see about that if and when Vendisi shows up, won't we?'

Kelsey made no move to follow her, and the upper floor was shrouded in silence when Lee crossed the inner edge of the living room and made her way upstairs. She had already changed for bed and was comfortably installed in its double width when she heard a door click opposite.

There was something alien about the thought of Kelsey being just the width of two walls away from her, getting ready for bed, lying alone in it, perhaps thinking about his unemotional guest. Had he imagined that, because she had accepted his invitation to stay at his island home, she would be open to a romantic interlude on the side? Lee smiled wryly into the room lit softly by starlight that drifted in through windows whose curtains she had drawn back. How much of a blow to his ego had it been when she remained cold in his arms? He must know his own attraction for women, and given the elastic moral standard of the world today he had probably taken it for granted that she would be open to a casual affair, no strings attached.

A frown bit down softly between her brows as she turned restlessly on her pillows. She didn't want any affair, casual or otherwise, with Kelsey Roberts. The life of emotional coolness she had lived for the past six years had been reached by suppressing the instincts he had roused so wantonly in her girlish self. She had no fears that she would make him the centre of her life again; tonight's session, when she had felt nothing, had shown her that. But life could be difficult on Madrona Island if he persisted in initiating scenes such as the one in the basement recreation room tonight. There must be somewhere she could go close by where she could await this Harry Vendisi's arrival.

She had fallen to sleep before she came to any rock-hard decision, but by the time she went downstairs the next morning she had made up her mind.

Kelsey was finishing breakfast in the small sitting room when she found him eventually, and she ignored his open appraisal of her royal blue shirt blouse and white tailored slacks as she helped herself to coffee and took the seat opposite his.

'Good morning, did you sleep well?' he asked, nothing in his genial host attitude to suggest that he remembered the previous evening.

'Good morning—yes, thanks.' Lee stirred cream and sugar into the coffee and drank thirstily, the peripheral area of her vision registering his handsome good looks in chest-hugging navy knit shirt and lighter blue slacks. 'I slept beautifully, it's so quiet here.'

'Nothing on your mind?' he said blandly, raising his cup to drain the coffee.

'Of course not. What should be on my mind?'

'I wondered if I—came on too strong last night.'

Lee looked up sharply, wondering if her ears were hearing what she imagined. Kelsey sounded almost contrite, almost——

Her laugh was a dismissing tinkle. 'Of course not. I'm used to men anxious to fill what they think is a deprived area of my life. You're no exception.'

'And you never accept what they're offering?'

There was a pregnant silence, broken when Freda came in and smilingly asked what she would like for breakfast.

'A lightly boiled egg, toast and coffee,' Lee ordered crisply.

'Sure you wouldn't like ham or bacon and eggs?' the housekeeper cajoled. 'It's no trouble.'

'What I've asked for will be fine.' Lee felt a momentary spasm of remorse when the housekeeper's face closed up at her brusque reply. 'I'd love some more of that delicious coffee right now, if you wouldn't mind.'

Partially mollified, Freda refilled her cup and Kelsey's before bustling off to prepare Lee's breakfast.

'I've been thinking,' Lee said brightly, stirring sugar into the capacious breakfast cup, 'that I'd like to see more of this corner of the world while I'm here. I thought I might spend a few days in Victoria. You can let me know when Mr Vendisi is likely to make his appearance and I'll come back here then. It seems a shame to hide out here on an island when there's so much to see elsewhere.' In face of Kelsey's silence, she prattled on, 'I seldom have the chance to vacation, and I'm not likely to be in this area again, so I——'

'I'll take you to Victoria, if that's what you want,' Kelsey interrupted morosely, black brows almost meeting above his dark eyes. 'I'll call the Empress and make arrangements for an overnight stay.'

Lee felt a suffocating sense of confinement and lifted her head with a hard-stared jerk. 'There's no need for you to come with me, I'm quite capable of taking care of myself.'

'I'm sure you are,' he conceded smoothly, 'but it's always better to see a place in the company of someone who knows it. If you'll excuse me, I'll go and make the arrangements now.'

Without waiting for her assent or otherwise, he pushed back his chair and went with his lean-hipped strides to the door. Meeting Freda there, he stood back politely while the housekeeper advanced with Lee's breakfast tray.

'I did your egg for four minutes, Mrs Whitney,' she said fussily as she arranged the food before Lee. 'I hope that's how you like it.'

'I usually have it done for three and a half minutes,' Lee said, taking out her irritation with Kelsey on the innocently obliging Freda, and immediately regretting her sourness. 'But I'm sure this will be fine,' she added hastily.

The egg could have been boiled to rock-hardness for all she tasted of it. Kelsey had virtually informed her that she was a prisoner on this island of his, only to venture beyond it in his overweening presence. Did Frantug—or, more likely, the Vendisi deal—mean that much to him?

Her business nose was twitching with interest at the Vendisi operation, and the last thing she would do was to let someone else get a head start on what might prove to be a profitable deal for Whitney. From what Kelsey had told her last night, it could be just that with the proper management. A deal which would be shared by the Roberts Corporation, necessitating a closeness of contact she would have been happier without, but . . . business was business.

'I've arranged for an overnight stay at the Empress tomorrow night,' Kelsey announced abruptly, coming back into the room but not sitting down. 'We'll leave in the morning, so you can see something of the Island while we drive down there.'

By the way he said 'Island' Lee knew that he referred to the large body of land which, to his small island, was the mainland.

'Thank you, but as I said, there's no need for you to come with me,' she responded coolly, biting unconcernedly into the crisp brown toast Freda had brought for her. 'I'm quite capable of seeing the sights without an escort.'

'As it happens, I have to be in Victoria on business the day after tomorrow, so there's no question of wasting my time, if that's what's bothering you.'

That hadn't been her problem, but Lee gave him an acknowledging nod. The claustrophobia she had felt closing in on her the day before was even more pronounced this morning because, she told herself, she wasn't used to the idea of time hanging heavily on her hands. The ordered symmetry of her life was thrown out of kilter by the prospect of endless days spent in idleness. Particularly days spent in the company of a Kelsey who was immune from the darts of revenge she had always planned for him when they met again.

'I have a few things to see to now, but I'd like to show you around the island later,' he said now, still in that remote voice that told her he was displeased about something. Had his ego really been that dented by her turn-down the night before? The wry thought occurred to her that rejection wasn't something a man like Kelsey was used to, especially in his personal relationships.

'Don't worry about me,' she said airily, finishing the last of her coffee and pushing back her chair. 'I can find my own way around.'

'All right,' he said with unexpected bluntness, 'I'll

see you at lunch time.' While Lee was still gathering her thoughts, he went from the room, leaving it inexplicably lonely.

But loneliness was a factor she had long ago come to terms with, and after renewing her light covering of lipstick in her room Lee made her way down through the house again and out on to the brick patio fronting it. The sea was calm again this morning, especially in the lagoon-shaped harbour where she had come ashore yesterday. The pier was bereft of boats, apart from a weathered-looking rowboat tied up close to the small curve of sand beach. She was, virtually, a prisoner on Kelsey's island.

The thought followed her as she stepped down from the terraced gardens, brilliant and sweetly smelling of flowers, and made her way to the side of the house visible from her upstairs bedroom. The grass was cut meticulously short here as on the front lawns, curving and receding as it touched and swerved away from the thick growth of forest at its edge. A rough path, wide enough for one person, meandered off through the trees. Not a path she would like to pursue, Lee told herself with a shiver, and directed her steps towards the more open rear area.

Sheer beauty greeted her there, so eye-catching that her steps slowed and stilled altogether as she took in the garden that had an old-world air with its tumbling roses supported by white trellises, the profusion of flowers she couldn't begin to name in swooping borders and individual beds. But it was a kidney-shaped pool, surrounded by huge pots brimming with vari-coloured flowers, that attracted her attention.

The sparkling water, toned to an azure blue reflected from its sides and bottom, looked more than
inviting. A pool largely unused, if only Kelsey was in
the habit of visiting the island. She stepped lightly
across the flower-bordered lawn and stared pen-
sively into the deceptive depth of the pool. Did even
Kelsey use it? His brother and sister-in-law didn't
care for the island, Freda had told her, so it couldn't
have been installed for their benefit.

Sun, rising behind the screen of trees beyond the
pool's perimeter, glinted off the blue-hazed water. It
was just as well that Kelsey's family shunned the
island. His head injuries might have blocked off his
memory, but Dorothy would be sure to remember the
girl she had routed from Kelsey's bed that morning in
San Francisco. Women didn't forget things like that.

'Good morning, ma'am.'

Lee jumped, so immersed in her thoughts that
another human's presence in this garden of Eden
startled her. A middle-aged man, his tall lean body
covered in workmanlike denim, stood just behind her
arcing a spray of water over the terracotta pots lining
the apron of the pool.

'Oh, good morning.' She should have known that
such meticulously cared for gardens were the product
of a skilled gardener, which this man looked to be.

'Beautiful day, ma'am, isn't it?'

Something about his accent prompted Lee's 'You
must be related to Freda,' and he chuckled, directing
the hose to the outlying pots.

'I certainly hope so, we've been married for nearly
thirty years.'

'You work as a team for Mr Roberts?'

'That's right, ma'am. Freda looks after the inside, and I take care of the outside.'

'Oh, I see. I was just thinking what a shame it is that such a beautiful pool should go to waste.'

Freda's mate laughed again. 'It doesn't go to waste while Mr Kelsey's here. He needed exercise to get back into shape after the accident, so he used the pool a lot when he was recuperating last year. Still does,' he offered laconically. 'Not many mornings go by but he's here swimming a few lengths. Then he'll often go in again before he has his dinner.'

'But not last night,' Lee said without thinking.

'No, but you were here, ma'am, weren't you? It's the first time he's missed in a long time, but then you're the first lady he's brought here since the accident.'

'Were there others before then?'

Obviously feeling he was getting in over his head, the gardener switched a lever on the hose in his hand and the water dripped to a stop. 'It was none of my business who Mr Kelsey chose to bring here, ma'am,' he informed her abruptly. 'All I can say is that his wife never came with him. This was, like, his own hideaway, and he came here to relax.'

Relax, Lee thought drily as the gardener moved off to another area. It didn't need any kind of super intelligence to know that Kelsey had relaxed in a way familiar to him—in a way he had expected to relax last night with her. No wonder he had been so curt this morning! His well laid schemes of seduction had gone sadly astray as far as she was concerned.

Leaving the pool behind, she ventured beyond its

encircling trees and found a tar-surfaced tennis court and a space dedicated to badminton beside it. Stretching beyond that, reaching to the iridescent blue of the ocean, was what seemed like a miniature golf course with its smoothly cut grass and breeze-tossed flags indicating the holes.

A sportsman's paradise, she mocked inwardly, hands on hips as she surveyed the amenities spread out behind and before her. And indoor pursuits when the occasion called for them. How many women had Kelsey initiated into the pleasures of golf, tennis, badminton, pool, not to mention the indoor activities he obviously excelled at? Activities like kissing, making love to the woman he had brought here, expecting and no doubt receiving her ardent response.

Lee swivelled on her heel and went back towards the house, which lay dozing in the full force of the August sun. What did it matter to her how many women he entertained on his island paradise? The kind of woman Kelsey would bring here would be confident, her eyes fully open, not a green eighteen-year-old with eyes filled with stardust, believing. . . .

CHAPTER FOUR

THE hotel's grand foyer, redolent with the atmosphere of a Victorian age long past, struck an unexpected note of homesickness in Lee as she walked through the teeming lobby. Something about the high-backed chairs, and the Oriental touch of wicker fan-shaped chairs arranged around small round tables where visitors were taking tea, was all too reminiscent of one or two San Francisco hotels and the homes of long-established families in that city.

'Heavens,' she gasped, buffeted by a long line of tourists awaiting their turn for tea, 'is this the only café in town?'

Kelsey gave a fleeting, and devastatingly handsome, smile, his fingers tightening on her elbow. 'Not the only one by a long way,' he said, wryly amused. 'But saying you've had tea and crumpets at the Empress scores a lot higher than saying you've had it at Phil's Eaterie.' His commanding presence at the desk brought immediate attention from a desk clerk who looked not in the least Victorian with her expertly applied make-up and professionally styled hair.

'Yes, of course, Mr Roberts. Your rooms are ready, I'll just try to find a bellhop for you.'

'No need for that, we just have overnight bags,' Kelsey told her with another smile that seemed to completely demoralise her. 'If you'll give me the keys, we'll find our own way up.'

Both rooms were on the fourth floor, though at different ends of the carpeted corridor. Lee's looked out over the front entrance to the Inner Harbour and, to her left, the turn-of-the-century Parliament Buildings taking pride of place amid emerald lawns and brightly coloured flower beds.

Turning back from the bank of windows overlooking the view, Lee said briskly, 'This is fine, though I would have liked to be a little higher.'

Kelsey stared at her, more familiar to her in dark jacket and tie than he had been in the casual garb of the island. A sardonic smile twisted his lips as he said,

'Do you know how lucky we are to find two separate rooms at the height of the season? This hotel is usually booked solid at this time of the year. It's only because——' he shrugged, and Lee filled in for him acidly,

'Because you have pull in these quarters?'

'I was about to say,' he returned quietly, 'that we were lucky they had a couple of cancellations.'

'Oh.' Lee paced back towards the two double-sized beds covered in elaborately scrolled gold bedspreads. 'Well, I suppose you want to get settled into your room,' she suggested pointedly, uncomfortable with the thoughts rising unbidden from somewhere inside her. If those adolescent dreams of hers had come true, she would be sharing this room with Kelsey, and only one of the full-size beds would be used.

'Yes,' he said, uncompromising as he strode back to the outer door. 'I'll pick you up in half an hour and we'll start seeing the sights.'

His capable shoulders filled the doorway momentarily and then he was gone. Lee turned back towards the windows, gazing unseeing at the active scene unfolding before her eyes. Shipping plied busily across the harbour, tourists strolled in holiday leisure along the causeway fronting the hotel, but she saw nothing of them. In other circumstances . . . how she hated those words! If her juvenile hopes had come to pass, Kelsey would be here with her now, sharing this room too large for one, showing her this part of the world which he knew and loved.

Love . . . such a fleeting emotion, yet there were people who lived by it all their lives. People who set down roots in the family they created together, children born of love and cherished because they were part of the other.

Giving a visible shrug, Lee moved away from the window and speedily unpacked the few necessities she had brought for the overnight visit . . . nightdress, white linen short-sleeved dress, toilet articles and cosmetics. Making a spur-of-the-moment decision, she stepped out of the cerulean blue pantsuit she had worn on their trip from the island and substituted the white dress. She doubted if there would be time to change again before dinner, and the dress was suitable for both sightseeing and the evening meal.

Kelsey came when the half hour was barely up, casual in cream silk polo neck shirt and midbrown slacks. Whatever he wore, Lee thought as she followed him from the room, he was every woman's dream of an attractive man. Not classically good-looking—his features were too individually carved for that—but he exuded attraction from every pore.

Even the middle-aged matron he waved solicitously
into the elevator before him fluttered her sandy eyelashes in his direction as they were borne speedily
down to the lobby.

'I thought we'd start with a horse-drawn tour,' he
said, taking possessive hold on her elbow as they
walked through the less crowded lobby to the wide
shallow entrance steps overlooking the harbour area.
'Victoria's a small place, so it doesn't take much
longer than an hour and a quarter, and you'll see
everything in a more leisurely fashion than you would
in a car.'

'That sounds fine.' Lee strove to find the unemotional calm she had brought to a fine art, but the
touch of Kelsey's fingers on her skin had a violent
effect that stole breath from her body and left her arm
with the feeling of having been scourged by white-hot
embers.

The horse-drawn wagons, each seating about two
dozen volubly excited tourists, were lined up not far
from the hotel, whose ivy-covered walls serenely
dominated the harbour view. Drawing her back,
Kelsey directed her to the next wagon in line, one
where their seats were in pride of position beside the
driver. Red Indian blankets were neatly folded on
each seat and Lee turned questioningly to Kelsey.

'Blankets? On a day like this?'

'It can get cool along the sea-front,' Kelsey told
her, 'but for now you can sit on it.' As if setting an
example, he levered his long form on to the bench
seat and stretched his legs as far as the front board
would permit. The two horses hitched to the wagon

waited patiently, ears flicking at the occasional both-
ersome fly, for their human cargo to board the increasingly weighty wagon. The driver, a young man
dressed in the blue jean/casual shirt style of young
men everywhere, at last came to take control of the
patiently waiting horses.

A childish thrill of anticipation ran through Lee as
the wagon jerked and set off in slow motion before the
majestic Parliament Buildings, spread in lazy splendour on their left, a statue of the queen from which
the city took its name facing tranquilly the seat of
democracy for British Columbia. The wagon guide,
his accent more reminiscent of England than North
America, proved to be a witty raconteur of Victoria's
past and recent history.

The Parliament Buildings, studded with light
bulbs to outline their splendour at night, were, he
told them, the seat of government for the Province of
British Columbia; the light bulbs, he added, were
reputedly made without the planned obsolescence of
manufacturing in today's world, and none had had to
be replaced since their installation several decades
before.

'This must be boring for you,' Lee glanced quickly
up at Kelsey's emphatically moulded profile, surprised to see the relaxed line of his mouth as the
paired horses drew them past a perpetual flame dominating a half-circle of Provincial emblems. 'You
must have seen all this a million times.'

'As a matter of fact, I haven't,' he smiled wryly
into her eyes. 'I know Victoria only in a superficial
way, as I'm sure a lot of the residents here do. Can

you say that you know everything about historic San Francisco?'

'No,' she admitted with an unexpectedly impish chuckle. Something about this wagon trip made her feel that way . . . lighthearted, with an almost childish appreciation for new wonders. Kelsey's arm dropped lower on the wooden seat back and lay lightly over her shoulders, but that seemed perfectly in accord with the strangely detached mood she had slipped into with surprising ease. How long had it been since she had been entirely free like this with no pressing obligations of business clouding her sight? Whitney Enterprises might not have existed, a remarkable feat in itself, as they wended their leisurely way along a clifftop sea-front made beautiful by the bright gold of broom and perennial wild flowers against a backdrop of crystal blue sea and snow-covered peaks of the Olympic mountain range which brought the United States more intimately close than Lee had imagined.

The rest of the ride, taken through the elegant flowerbeds and restrained entertainment areas of Beacon Hill Park, passed in a dream for Lee. In an odd way, time had been suspended and she took uncritical pleasure in the sight of ecstatic toddlers being pushed in swings by doting mothers, the white-clad men slowly playing cricket on a sun-browned pitch, the velvet putting green surrounded by trees and garden beds of brilliant flowers. It was as if she were young again, like the young couples strolling closely entwined across the picturesque bridge spanning the lake . . . in love again, as they were.

Nothing in the rest of the afternoon's itinerary dispelled that sense of unreality. It was as if Kelsey catered to the wondering child in her—the magic of Sealand with Haida, the mammoth whale performing tricks designed to soften the hardest heart, and Miracle, the baby whale rescued from sure death by man-made wounds and nursed to health in the commandeered pool of a local hotel. Lee followed where Kelsey led her, and there was nothing alarming to her in the light, dry hold of his hand in the Provincial Museum where they viewed the natural history of the province and moved on to the re-creation of Victorian times with its plushly furnished hotel room, telegraph office and fashion stores circa the year 1800.

'Did they really have waists that small?' Lee pondered, her gaze fixed on a ruffled and laced model.

'Why not?' Kelsey returned goodhumouredly, his eyes appraising as they went over the figure-defining white of her dress. 'I reckon you'd be able to fit into that dress without too much trouble.'

'Only if my waist was tied in to eighteen inches by one of those stays they used to wear,' Lee retorted smartly, moving on to a display of horrific-looking surgeon's tools in use a century before. Why had she been so pleased by his comment, obviously meant as a compliment? Surely women had progressed enough since those days to not need the artificial torture of stays that bound their internal organs and made them incapable of eating a normal sized meal? But something of that bygone age's ambience followed them as they moved from one exhibit to the other. What would it have been like to be married to a man

like Kelsey in those days? Days when men were men
and women were—what? Chattels? Women who
lived lives of iron self-will which precluded any de-
viation from the morality they had been imbued with
since birth? Yes, of course. Women then had subdued
the sensual parts of their nature, making it easier for
them to accept the peccadilloes of their husbands.

Finding that thought too close to home, Lee made
no objections when Kelsey suggested that they make
their way to the rooftop restaurant where he had
made reservations for dinner.

'The restaurant is named for a woman who lived
on this site years ago,' Kelsey explained as they took
their seats beside windows giving a panoramic view of
the waterfront area and the towering majesty of the
Olympics in the background. He went on conversa-
tionally when the waiter had taken their order for
drinks. 'She was an eccentric who kept parrots, and
eventually her place become known as the Parrot
House. Hence the name of the restaurant.'

'It's nice that the hotel developers called it that in
memory of a landmark of Victoria,' Lee commented
coolly, her fingers nervously rearranging the gleam-
ing cutlery laid out before her. Despite a renovating
visit to the powder room, she had to restrain her hand
forcibly from reaching up to smooth the already spar-
tan drawback of her hair. Where had her cool persona disappeared to? Was one short afternoon in
Kelsey's company sufficient to demolish the careful
construction of her personality?

Obviously it was, she told herself drily, noting the
slight shaking of her fingers as she twined them round

the long-stemmed glass the waiter brought at that moment. But she stared down at the pale liquid of her Martini for long moments before lifting it to her lips. There had been a hollow inside her, a vacuum previously filled with the slow-burning fires of revenge, ever since she had discovered that Kelsey had not only lost his wife in a car accident, but that he himself had blank spaces in his memory—one of them being his fleeting affair with the naïve girl Lee had been seven years ago. Yet the woman she was now was far removed from that girl . . . she didn't love him any more. That much had been proved by the abortive love scene between them at the pool table.

'Are your thoughts private, or can anyone join in?' Kelsey's voice, lightly bantering, broke the spell.

'My thoughts are usually private, aren't yours?' she retorted crisply.

'Most of the time, yes,' he returned mildly, 'but it helps occasionally to share a problem with someone sympathetic.' A brief smile touched his dark-lashed eyes. 'And from the size of that frown you're wearing, I imagine you have a pretty big problem on your mind.'

Lee drank swiftly from her glass before saying, her eyes fixed frostily on his across the table, 'I'm used to working out any problems I have on my own, Mr Roberts. I've never found it necessary, or wise, to confide in other people, however—sympathetic they might be.'

His mouth formed a wry twist. 'Are you really that self-sufficient? Or are you just scared of intimate contact?'

'Scared? Don't be ridiculous!' Lee's voice held a tremulousness she hated as she went on scathingly, 'Do you think a person running scared would have been able to build up and run a highly successful corporation? You should know better than that, Mr Roberts.'

'You've just proved my point,' he observed in quiet triumph. 'Being able to relate to people has nothing to do with business acumen or the lack of it. You can't even bring yourself to use my given name, although I've asked you to do so.'

Glaring, Lee half spluttered, 'Kelsey, then! Does that satisfy you?'

'I'd prefer it said with a little less aggression, but it's not bad for a start.' He picked up the thick leather menu with maddening nonchalance. 'Shall we choose what we want to eat? There's somewhere I want to take you later.'

He bent his head, and Lee was left looking impotently at the thick smooth sideways parting of his hair. From innocently enjoyable afternoon to questionable discotheque evening!

'I don't care for noisy nightclubs,' she said unnecessarily loudly, and stared frigidly at an attractive woman at the next table who looked at her and then, significantly, at Kelsey.

Briefly, he looked up. 'Did I say I was taking you to a nightclub? Why can't you trust me to know what would appeal to you?'

His head dipped again, while Lee fumed on a different tack. Trust him! Hadn't she trusted him seven years ago, and with what result? Trust had been ground to ashes in the shame and bewilderment she had felt after finding out that he was married, not free to love her in the way she had girlishly expected. Thank God she was no longer that starry-eyed girl! Her life was mapped out now as a fully mature woman, without the blinkers of sentimentality to obscure her view. She needed no man to bolster her sense of self-worth; the world of commerce was her husband, subsidiary deals her children. If she felt the need for marriage, there was Maitland who would make no unrealistic demands on her time or emotions.

Her surprise showed visibly when, after the meal, they descended to the ground floor and Kelsey, hand firmly at her elbow, directed her towards the harbour area where lights twinkled on the cruisers berthed there and on their left the Parliament Buildings were outlined in lights, giving their bulk the impression of a fairyland castle awaiting the arrival of a princess.

Other people strolled as they did along the flower-decked lower causeway beside the boats anchored on a glass-calm sea, families taking a last breath of air before retiring to their motels and hotels close by, couples with arms entwined oblivious to the world around them. The slide of Kelsey's arm from elbow to waist was hardly noticeable, and Lee relaxed against his arm, finding herself caught up again in the simple magic of that afternoon's sightseeing. An alien pang of envy shot through her when they passed, so close that she could have touched them, a young couple so absorbed in the kiss they were sharing that their world was encompassed in their two straining figures.

'I'm sorry,' Lee said in a voice that was almost a whisper. She sensed Kelsey's head turning down towards hers.

'For what?'

'I thought you'd want a noisy discotheque instead of this.'

'Would I spend every minute I can on Madrona Island if that's what I like?' he put drily, halting in the shadows at the far end of the walkway to pull her round to face him. 'We like the same things, Lee. Doesn't that mean anything to you?'

'What should it mean?'

'Maybe this,' he said huskily, bending his head so quickly that Lee had no time to utter more than a startled gasp that left the soft outline of her lips parted as his mouth claimed hers.

Something in the night air, the warm ambience of their surroundings, left Lee with her defences down. Unwittingly her mouth acquiesced to the instant demand of his as it searched, probed, crushed the petal softness of her lips and re-lit a flame that had burned so brightly between them years before. Her heightened senses were aware of the shaved harshness of his chin, the wine flavour of his breath on hers, the heavy touch of his chest against hers, the piercing outline of his trouser belt on the tender outline of her stomach.

A flood of physical desire rose in her and swept away the barriers she had painstakingly erected between herself and the primitive joys she had known once in her life. Like a desert man deprived of water for too long, Lee responded to the throbbing beat in her inflamed veins and surrendered willingly, joyously, to the heady excitement Kelsey provoked. Like the girl of the couple they had recently passed, she pressed the slender line of her body to the overwhelming need in Kelsey's, drowned in the sensations that caught her up and whirled her beyond control to the world she had glimpsed once, long ago. . . .

'Lee . . . oh, Lee,' Kelsey groaned at her ear, his mouth warm from hers, 'I knew you couldn't be the cold woman you seemed the other night. Let's go back to the hotel, hmm?'

'Yes,' she whispered breathlessly at his neck, a neck warm and vital under her softly kissing lips. It couldn't end like this, when her blood cried out for a repeat of the fulfilment she had once known with him. She wanted to be with him, know him again, as a woman ultimately knows a man. The sensuous touch of his hand on her hip punctuated their walk back to the imposing ivy-covered hotel, and Lee walked in a rosy haze which acknowledged nothing but the coursing demands of her veins. She loved Kelsey, had always loved Kelsey; what did it matter that he remembered nothing of their previous liaison? His wife was dead now, incapable of being hurt by a casual affair her husband might indulge in. . . .

Casual affair. The words penetrated Lee's euphoric feeling as they entered the elevator, Kelsey's hand still firmly at her waist, his eyes still darkly liquid from the physical desire which had flared between them.

Lee felt the clouds of illusion dissipate and roll into oblivion as they walked closely together down the

corridor leading to her room. What was happening
here?

She was giving in to the sentimentality she had
long denied in herself. The effect Kelsey had exerted
over her that moonlit tranquil night meant no more
to him than the casual seduction of an eighteen-year-
old girl who had fallen, mesmerised, for his practised
charm seven years before. How stupid could she be?
She, who had loved wisely but not well, was on the
brink of committing the same mistake again. As a
person, she meant nothing to Kelsey. No more than
the bright-eyed teenager he had crassly seduced all
those years before.

'Thank you for a lovely day,' she said formally
outside her door, ignoring the decisive frown slicing
down between Kelsey's dark brows as he faced her
across the doorway. 'Did you have anything in mind
for the morning?'

'Nothing at all,' he gritted sandily, then he took a
step closer to her. 'What the hell's going on, Lee? Just
a few minutes ago you were as warm as any woman
I've ever known. Now you're acting like an ice
maiden—why?'

Lee allowed an icy curve to her mouth. 'Maybe
because I'm not a starry-eyed teenager, Mr
Roberts—Kelsey,' she mocked. 'You really must play
havoc with the hearts of children.'

'I've never been in the habit of seducing children,
if that's what you're implying,' he returned stiffly,
seeming to withdraw from her although his body was
still squarely set before her.

Anger shot vitriol through Lee's veins. 'Aren't you,

Kelsey? You don't seem to me the kind of man who would have too many scruples about taking advantage of innocence.'

His body tensed visibly, and his eyes sparked a dark violence, but his voice came out evenly when he said, 'You've known me three days. Do you feel that gives you the right to judge my moral character?'

Lee's glinting blue eyes were the first to break contact. Her lashes swept down obscuring the bitter knowledge they held. 'Men can be as easy to read as a book, and your type is in large easy-to-read print!'

'And you're an expert?' he mocked, leaning sideways against the doorway, regarding her with cynical eyes. 'Strange, from what I've discovered about you I'd have said you know very little about men and the less savoury aspects of their character, even though you've been married.' His voice changed to deep mockery. 'But then you married an old man, didn't you, Lee? A man who wasn't likely to make the demands a younger husband would have—was that his attraction? Or was it solely his money?'

Lee's swift lift of her hand was automatic, the meeting of palm against lean face momentarily satisfying. 'How dare you be so presumptuous?' she blazed, an anger that was real shaking her to her bones. 'Fletcher Whitney was a gentleman, someone a man like you would find hard to understand. I married him because he was kind and understanding, and I loved him.'

Kelsey straightened from the doorpost and gave her a mock bow, the hard line of his cheek reddened from her blow. 'I apologise for the bit about marrying him for his money, but not about the April-December aspect of it. No man in his sixties could have satisfied the needs of a beautiful teenage girl.'

The fact that he was right did nothing to assuage Lee's towering force of anger. 'There's more to marriage than the purely physical,' she snapped, bending the indignant line of her neck as she reached for the room key in her bag. Her splutter of surprise went unnoticed when Kelsey took the key from her and applied it to the door, swinging it open and ushering her ungently into the room before closing it with a decisive click behind them.

'Please leave my room,' she said, her voice icily hard. 'Or do I have to call the hotel desk?'

'You can call whoever you like in ten minutes from now,' Kelsey told her grimly, drawing her by the arm farther into the room and detaching her handbag to throw it on the nearer bed, where it slid down the gold spread to lie on the floor. 'In the meantime I'm going to prove to you that kindness and understanding are fine, but they're not all of marriage either.'

There was no time to protest as his arms jerked her to the hard line of his body, no possibility of voicing the protest as his mouth impacted on hers. Stunned, Lee was no more capable of rejecting his kiss than of breaking free from the steel bands his arms formed around her. She was conscious only of a dark force driving like iron into her body, searing, burning, sweeping aside every barrier she had staunchly erected as if each one had been made of flimsy cardboard.

Opening her lips to protest when Kelsey relaxed his hold slightly, she found them plundered again by the piercing warmth of his, and the futile movements of rejection she made only seemed to draw her into closer contact with the forceful arc of his body. His hands augmented the message of his mouth, flaming her flesh under the white of her dress wherever they touched. Desire flickered and grew to a blaze, fed by the hunger she had rigidly controlled for so long.

Unable to deny that starvation of her senses, her body curved and pressed to the shape of his, her arms rising to rest on the broad line of his shoulders, her mouth eager as it clung to his.'

'Lee . . . oh, Lee,' Kelsey breathed at her ear, his lips warm as they pressed the line of her throat to the hollow at its base, 'let me stay with you . . . love you. . . .'

'Yes,' she whispered, everything forgotten in the pounding beat of her thundering pulses, 'oh, yes, Kelsey!'

Afterwards she could never remember how they reached the bed, only the silken feel of her skin as Kelsey caressed it, rousing the dormant passion she had thought never to know again. The smooth, warm hardness of his flesh was familiar, like a vivid and half forgotten dream. His mouth, as it traversed the curves and indentations of her figure, almost worshipful in its appreciation of her female beauty.

'Kelsey,' his name formed on her breath, lost in the swift descent of his mouth that engulfed hers in a wordless need that transcended the passage of years, as new and thrilling to Lee as that first coming to-gether had been. She loved him, just as surely as she had. . . .

The telephone between the beds jangled un-bearably, splintering the almost monastic silence in the room, stiffening their bodies to unwilling alert-ness.

'Who the hell is that?' Kelsey swore viciously, trapping the hand Lee reached out to the cream-coloured instrument on the night table. 'Don't answer.'

Drawn abruptly back to her senses, Lee stared up into the dark glitter of his passionately lit eyes. What was she doing here, with Kelsey, like this? Her eyes went down to where his brown arm, thick with dark hairs, lay across the whiteness of her skin. What was she doing here with him like this? It was as if she had gone back in time to her teenage, when an experi-enced man like Kelsey had been able to overcome her teenage scruples with no trouble at all. He had done the same tonight . . . with no trouble at all.

'It might be something important,' she said huskily, reaching for the phone across his tanned torso. 'Yes?' she said into the receiver.

'Lee, is that you?' Maitland's voice came clearly across the line.

'Yes, it's me, Maitland.' She drew the coverlet across her when Kelsey rolled from her and sat on the edge of the bed. 'Is anything wrong?'

'Nothing, except that I was anxious that I hadn't heard from you.' Maitland's rich tones came across the line as if he were in the same room. 'How is everything going there?'

'Fine.' Lee made a swift mental comparison with Maitland's plumply solid physique and Kelsey's, her eyes resting on the bronzed toughness of muscle close to her. 'How did you know where to find me?'

'The housekeeper on the island said you were staying at the Empress with the Roberts man. Was it necessary for you to go there?'

Irritated by the possessively jealous tone in his voice, Lee said sharply, 'Of course. Would I be here otherwise?'

Maitland still seemed uncomfortable with the idea. 'I thought the shipping business was centred in Seattle and Vancouver.'

'It is,' Lee responded briskly. 'The principal isn't on the island as yet, so I decided to spend a little time sightseeing.'

'Sightseeing?' Maitland responded doubtfully. 'On your own?'

'Mr Roberts came with me.' Lee's eyes went to where Kelsey was encasing his bronzed body in the clothes he had discarded so rapidly.

'He's there with you?' Maitland questioned sharply.

'Yes.'

'Lee, I hope you're not being too friendly with that guy,' he came back plaintively. 'He could take it the wrong way—you know what I mean.'

'No, I don't,' Lee spoke coolly. 'Tell me.'

'Well, you're not exactly the girl next door, are you?' he protested, and Lee had a fleeting vision of his pink face coloured by embarrassment to red. 'You have to be careful of men who wouldn't mind at all getting control of Whitney Enterprises.'

'I can take care of myself, Maitland,' she told him crisply, only peripherally aware of Kelsey's fully clad figure standing at the foot of the bed. 'Are you suggesting otherwise?'

'No, no, of course not,' he hastened to assure her. 'I just thought I should warn you.'

'There's no need.'

'Was that the boy-friend?' Kelsey asked derisively when she put the receiver back in its cradle.

'It was Maitland Frasier,' she admitted coolly, passion stripped from her as surely as Kelsey's donning of his clothes indicated that he was through with the amorous minutes preceding the phone call.

'Are you going to marry him?' Kelsey asked abruptly, his face an aloof mask of indifference.

'Perhaps.'

'Then you're a damn fool,' he told her raggedly, sweeping the thick blackness of his hair with his hand as he came to stand over her. 'I don't know him, but I'd bet my last dollar that he's no more suitable as a husband for you than your last one was.'

Leaving her gaping, he strode to the door and went through it, closing it with a definite bang behind him.

Paralysed by the thoughts filling her mind, Lee lay unmoving on the firm hotel mattress long after he had gone. Was he right? Or was it Maitland who had hit on the truth of the matter?

Kelsey had no memory of their fleeting affair years ago; to him, Lee was an attractive woman possessed of power and influence in the corporate world. Staring at the ceiling, she recalled his hungry need to gain control of Frantug all those years ago. Had he thought then that making love to Fletcher Whitney's assistant would enhance his chances of gaining that vital control?

Her mouth twisted wryly. Wouldn't he have much more to gain by making love to the President of Whitney Enterprises? Maybe even toying with the idea of marrying her, securing an assured future of corporate bliss.

Feeling coldly detached from her nude state, Lee raised herself from the bed and picked up the clothing Kelsey had discarded so impatiently. She took a shower, then, before donning the cobweb lightness of the pale green nightdress she had brought. Every movement was accompanied by the probing click of her brain. Was Kelsey motivated by the need to consolidate his interests in the shipping industry? She had control of Frantug, and the means to bring Harry Vendisi's import company into his orbit. In his position, she might have thought along the same lines. Business was business, even if it meant compromising personal integrity.

The muted sound of traffic came through the thickly curtained windows, but it was the thoughts circulating in her head that kept Lee awake and staring into the darkness. Why was it that Kelsey still seemed to have that mesmeric power over her? She had succumbed as readily to him tonight as she had all those years ago. But then there had been an excuse for her ... young, full of the romantic dreams of eighteen, bowled over by a man of experience who had his own star to follow. A star that seemingly hadn't changed over the intervening years. He wanted Frantug, and he wanted the Vendisi shipping business. Nothing had changed. He was still using the same tactics to gain his ends.

Damn him! She moved restlessly under the covers, squirming in the knowledge that she had been no more worldly-wise that night than she had been at eighteen. Every part of her had yearned for his touch; the sensual outline of his mouth had left its erotic memory on her peaked breasts, the unassuaged longing deep in the pit of her stomach. Humiliation swamped her when she recalled the eagerness of her response to his lovemaking. It was as if she had been the starry-eyed girl of eighteen rather than the woman of business she knew herself to be. Kelsey appealed to the base physical core of her, the part devoid of other considerations. Her weakness lay there; all she had to do was to suppress that part of her vulnerability and victory would be hers.

Pondering the method of doing this, Lee fell into a troubled sleep.

CHAPTER FIVE

FREDA's excited eyes greeted them on the pier when Geoff laconically tied the cruiser to its capstans.

'Mr Vendisi's party is arriving this afternoon,' she addressed Kelsey. 'I've got rooms ready for them, but I really have to have some help in the kitchen, Mr Kelsey.'

'All right,' he placated, turning from helping Lee to shore to the agitated housekeeper. 'Get the girls we've used before from Duncan.'

'Most of them are busy right now in the hotels and motels there,' Freda returned worriedly. 'But I think I may be able to persuade my friend's daughter to help out. She's young, but at least she's willing.'

'Good for you,' Kelsey approved, standing aside for Lee to precede him on to the sandy path leading up to the house. 'What time is Mr Vendisi's party expected?'

Lee walked on while he discussed details with his housekeeper. Nothing was of less interest to her than the domestic details of running Kelsey's island paradise.

What narrowed her eyes to a speculative line was the knowledge that Harry Vendisi was at last to honour the island with his visit—and that of a woman companion, if the disjointed phrases floating in the air behind her were correct.

'I've put him and Mrs Vendisi in the room overlooking the pool,' Freda told him. 'I hope they won't mind twin beds.'

Kelsey's chuckle reached clearly to Lee's ears. 'I doubt very much if it's Mrs Vendisi who's accompanying him, Freda.'

'Oh,' she sounded nonplussed, then vaguely annoyed as she went on, 'Oh, dear, then I'll have to find another room for the lady.'

'There's no need for that,' Kelsey returned easily. 'They're used to sharing when he travels.'

Lee inwardly echoed Freda's startled gasp, but whereas the housekeeper's surprise was motivated by shocked morality, her own sprang from Kelsey's easy acceptance of the situation. Yet why should she be surprised? She had learned long ago that his ethical sense did not stretch to encompass marital fidelity. Vendisi's being accompanied by a woman not his wife was no more than a source of amusement to him.

He caught up with her on the brick patio leading into the house, the familiar clasp of his fingers round her wrist making her swing round to stare at him with frigid blue eyes.

'Will you act as hostess for me while Harry and his—companion are here?' he asked, the relaxed smile fading from his mouth when he noted her hostility. 'It could be a lucrative deal for both of us.'

'What does that mean? That I'm supposed to exert my female charms on the man from the underworld so that he'll give us a good deal? What would his "companion" think of that?'

Kelsey's eyes narrowed. 'There are limits. I wasn't suggesting you hop into bed with him, just that you show a little more warmth than you normally do. I wouldn't care to see it extended beyond that.'

'*You* wouldn't care to see it extended?' she repeated incredulously. 'You're not my keeper, nor are you my business manager! I'm quite capable of making my own deals without your interference.'

'You'll make no deals unless I'm in on them,' Kelsey gritted, harshly male in his wide-legged stance before her. 'You don't know Vendisi's type.'

'Perhaps not,' Lee retorted, stepping backwards towards the opened patio doors, 'but I have a healthy regard for Whitney Enterprises, and I don't make decisions lightly. He'll deal on my terms or not at all.'

She escaped into the house, walking with fluidly rapid steps across the living room/hall and gaining the red-carpeted stairs to the upper floor. From the wide gallery with its view into the living room below she saw Kelsey, his shoulders uncharacteristically drooping, draw the patio door shut and turn inward to the seating area.

How naïve did he think she was? The choleric thought followed her into the sumptuous suite he had put at her disposal, trailing her steps as they went to the dominating view exposed by the bank of sitting-room windows. Less chaotic than her thoughts, the distant sea lay tranquil under the early afternoon sun, a sailboat drifting windlessly westward. Negotiating with Harry Vendisi, although she had never dealt with his type before, would be a lot easier than coping with a man like Kelsey. Vendisi would be brash, uncouth compared with the younger man's all too

obvious attractions, a person she could cope with on a
superior level. Not unlike some of the less polished
personalities she had met in business in San Francisco. She had long ago become used to hardbitten
tycoons dropping their brusque air of arrogant certainty in the presence of her level-eyed gaze. Her
father had not called her his 'little lady' with no
result. She had slipped into the role of Fletcher's wife
as simply as if wealth had been hers to command all
her life. Even Fletcher had been impressed by her
grace and dignity. . . .

Or was it her coldness? Lee turned from the
window abruptly. It hadn't been too hard to present
herself to San Francisco society as the young but
coolly collected wife of a man they respected. Her
outward appearance had only reflected the deadness
of her inner sensations. Nerves that had remained
numb until now, until she had met Kelsey Roberts
again.

Taking off the pantsuit she had worn on the return
trip from Victoria, Lee ran a scaldingly hot bath and
soaked in its scented fragrance for twenty minutes or
more. The steam wreathing up around her made her
hair damp, limp, but she shrugged that knowledge
off. There would be time later for that. . . .

. . . 'Lee! . . . Lee! . . . Wake up, Lee!'

The male voice, roughened with alarm, pierced
her misty consciousness, opening her eyes abruptly.
Her heart began to thump heavily in her breast as she
blinked at the shadowy figure that seemed to fill the
steamy bathroom. What was she doing here? More to
the point, what was Kelsey doing here in her bath-

room, staring down at her white-faced as if he had just been dealt a blow to the stomach?

Water, soft and warm, lapped under her chin and she sat up with a sudden movement that made chaotic waves on its still surface. God, she must have fallen asleep in the tub—but how, why? And why was Kelsey standing beside it with a wrath like that of the deity she had invoked?

'Wh—what are you doing in here?' she spluttered, belatedly aware that the water came up only as far as her waist and crossing defensive arms across the pink-tipped exposure of her breasts.

'Saving you from drowning,' Kelsey bit out harshly, then drew in a rasping breath of steamy air. 'What the hell do you think you're doing? Do you make a habit of falling asleep in your bath? If so, it amazes me that you're still around to tell the tale!'

'I've never fallen asleep in my bath,' she denied in a throaty voice that denied her statement. 'And you can save your gallant lifesaving gestures for somebody who needs them! Now will you please go and let me get out?'

'I'll not only let you get out, I'll help you!' Ignoring Lee's indignant gasp, Kelsey reached down and with bewildering speed lifted her dripping body from the cooled water to the thick plush of the bathmat. The white signs of strain disappeared from around his eyes as they dropped slowly down over the curves and indentations she vainly tried to cover. His voice instantly soft and thick, he murmured, 'You're even more beautiful than I—thought.'

An uncontrollable tremor rippled sickly down

Lee's spine. It wasn't possible—*couldn't* be possible—
that the sensations curling up from deep inside her
were caused by his nearness, his frank male appreciation of a woman's body he found desirable. Yet the
weakness spread insider her, reaching down to the
toes curling into the bathmat, up to swell the breath
in her throat. It was stupid, idiotic, to allow the feelings swamping her to drift up to her brain, dulling the
persistent small voice that told her she was a fool to let
herself become embroiled with a man like Kelsey
Roberts again.

'Kelsey, please!' her voice came out in an anguished croak when his arms lifted slowly and his
bronzed hands touched the alabaster white of her
shoulders. The spring-like tension that she sensed in
him was in her too, an explosive force that would
blow every barrier she had erected to atoms. How
could this be happening to her, who had been so
positive that nothing but hate could ever lie between
them? When Kelsey, his eyes clouded by an almost
reverential awe, murmured hoarsely, 'My God, Lee,
your skin is so soft, so white,' she groped desperately
for the unemotional coolness she had based her
actions on for so long.

'The sun doesn't reach the executive offices of
Whitney Towers,' she snapped, only a slight tremor
in her voice betraying that his touch moved her at all.
'Now will you please let me go? I don't care for being
on show to satisfy your male urges.'

She went to sidepass him, reaching for the towel
placed tantalisingly on the rail behind him, and
gasped when Kelsey's hand shot out to encircle her

wrist and jerk her body so hard against his that the breath was knocked from her.

'That wasn't how you felt last night, was it?' he ground out with a savagery that frightened her. The widened darkness of her blue eyes reflected the twin pools of black anger in his.

'I'm not proud of what happened last night,' she said, her lips tightening round the words which acknowledged a fact she would far rather ignore. Aware all at once of the potency of his grip that crushed the soft swell of her breasts to the hard warmth of his chest, she tried to twist out of his arms but found herself instead pressed more fully, and painfully, against him. To struggle more was not only undignified, but impossible. 'I—I wasn't myself.'

'No,' he jeered, his voice ugly as he stared down into her pale features, 'you were human last night. You reacted like a normal woman when a man makes love to her—until your corporate lover called you. Do you let the ice melt when you're in bed with him?'

Lee's head snapped up and she glared frostily into his glittering eyes. 'Not all men have your uncivilised animal instincts! Your kind wouldn't understand a man like Maitland.'

'Ain't that the truth,' Kelsey drawled the slow insult. 'I'd bet everything I have that he's never even asked for the privilege of sharing your bed.'

'No, he hasn't,' Lee flared, hating Kelsey more at that moment than she ever had before. 'And I wouldn't have expected him to.' Her blood seemed stemmed in the arm he still held relentlessly twisted behind her back, but to struggle would only tighten his grip. 'You're bruising my arm,' she said coldly.

He loosened his grip immediately, though his fingers still encircled her wrist loosely. 'Does he make love to you at all? Does he kiss you?' he pursued with a sickeningly persistent curiosity.

'That's nothing to do with you,' she spat out angrily, giving a futile twist that only anchored her more firmly against him. 'Why should it bother you?'

'It bothers me,' he said slowly, his eyes raking the cheeks flushed from indignation and the residue of steam in the bathroom, 'because I hate to see a good woman go to waste.' His hand suddenly left her wrist and came up to touch her face, his fingertips evocatively gentle as they traced her skin from cheekbone to chin. 'Such a waste,' he half crooned while Lee stared into his dark eyes like a small creature captured in a beaming headlight. 'He doesn't deserve you, any more than Fletcher Whitney did.'

Mention of Fletcher snapped her out of the hypnotic state his voice had reduced her to, and she jerked her head sideways, letting his hand fall to her throat's hollow.

'Don't foul his memory by speaking his name,' she gasped jerkily. 'He was the finest man who ever lived. . . .'

'But not one who made you feel like this,' Kelsey snapped, sliding his fingers up through her hair from her nape, loosening the pins that held it so that it fell damply around her face. His head moved, and his mouth ground with fine savagery on hers, shocking her with its impact and prompting the rigid stiffness of her spine.

A struggle, useless physically against his strength, went on chaotically inside her. Hatred coiled and released itself impotently through her veins, the harsh insult of abrasive male chin searing her tender flesh as Kelsey deepened the kiss. Her hands came up to pound uselessly against his unremitting chest and then lay still over the erratic thump of his heart.

Just when the black vitriol changed to the thick languor of gold creeping insidiously to her far reaches she couldn't afterwards recall. All she knew was that there was no fight in her any more, only the pressing need to bend like a reed to a man whose rough-handed caresses made her skin feel like spun silk.

'Lee,' he groaned, 'oh, Lee, why did you do it?' His lips branded searing kisses on her throat, her shoulders, breasts where they lingered achingly. 'I love——'

The agitated knocking on the outer door of the suite got through to them at the same time. Lee found herself holding her breath, her arms inexplicably wound round Kelsey's strongly columned neck, her slender body moulded to his as if they were one. A shiver ran over her when the knocking came again.

'Mrs Whitney? Are you all right?'

Abruptly, Kelsey released her and Lee was left swaying as he ripped the voluminous bath towel from the rail and folded it round her.

'You'd better explain that you were taking a bath,' he said tersely, running a smoothing hand over the ruffled thickness of his black hair. 'Lee?'

She turned obediently, bereft of individual thought, and felt Kelsey's hand on her arm.

'It's not for my sake. I don't give a damn if she knows I'm here in your bathroom.'

Nodding without understanding, Lee stepped barefoot from the bathroom and across the deeply carpeted floor and opened the outer door to an agitated Freda.

'Oh, Mrs Whitney, you're all right!' she gasped in relief. 'I wondered if something had happened to you.'

Lee seemed to speak through a wad of cotton in her throat. 'I—I'm fine, I was—taking a bath. Did you want me for something?'

Freda's brow knitted with concern. 'I was just wondering if you knew where Mr Kelsey might be. Mr Vendisi and his party arrived half an hour ago, and I can't seem to find Mr Kelsey anywhere.'

'I'm sure he'll turn up any minute now,' Lee told her breathlessly, stifling an hysterical laugh that bubbled up unexpectedly from deep in her throat. What would the straitlaced housekeeper think if she knew that at that moment Kelsey was skulking in the bathroom she herself had just come from?

'I certainly hope so. Mr Vendisi isn't too pleased that no one was here to greet him.' Freda half turned away, then looked back curiously at Lee's rose-flushed cheeks. 'I hope you haven't been taking a bath that's too hot,' she said severely. 'It can be dangerous, you know.'

'I know.'

How she knew! Without questioning the effervescent buoyancy that made her steps literally bounce on her way back to the bathroom, Lee drew up short at the sight of Kelsey's leanly spare body propped against the doorway.

'Your visitors have arrived,' she breathed softly, her eyes luminously tender as they took in the moulding contours of his blue denims, the white tee-shirt stained with her own dampness. 'I told——'

'I heard,' he interrupted brusquely, brushing past her on his way to the door. 'I'd like you to stay up here until I've had a chance to talk with Vendisi. Come down for drinks before dinner.'

Lee stared, her inner bewilderment reflected in the dark blue of her eyes. What was wrong with him? A few minutes ago he had been every woman's ideal of a lover, strong, forceful, desirous. It seemed now that with the fading of physical desire the coolly practical business man had taken control.

She was still standing in the same position minutes later, long after Kelsey had gone through the door and closed it decisively behind him. What a fool she was, an idiotic, blind fool to have succumbed to the sheer male charm of him. She had learned nothing from the bitter lesson he had taught her, not one thing. That was only too obvious; cringing inwardly at the memory of how quickly her façade of cool hatred had crumbled, Lee walked with stiff steps to the windows overlooking the side of the house, oblivious of the westering sun carving its golden inroad on the faintly restless ocean. Nothing had really changed; she still hated Kelsey, perhaps more so because of her own vulnerability to the physical attraction he exuded from every pore. All she had to do was to summon up the bitter gall that still lay like a pulsing presence deep inside her.

Vendisi was here ... what was wrong with her original plan to string him along in the expectation that she would join with Kelsey in taking over the shipping business Vendisi himself was no longer interested in? Backing out at the last minute would hurt no one but Kelsey. The business acumen that had carried Lee through the years after her marriage to Fletcher knew instinctively that this deal was important to Kelsey. More so than Frantug, than the shipping business he and his brother shared in Seattle.

Nothing had changed, she told herself firmly again. Only Kelsey knew of her momentary weakness, her purely physical reaction to him as a man. And even he would be disabused of that idea when she paid more flattering attention to Vendisi than to himself.

Turning quickly towards the closets flanking one side of the room, she looked appraisingly at the wardrobe she had brought with her.

Taking advantage of the unimpeded view of the downstairs living room, Lee paused at the entrance to the gallery passage. Unbidden, her eyes sought out and found Kelsey's dominant figure, his shoulders sleekly muscled in dark dinner jacket, his lean-featured face highlighted by the pristine white of a crisply laundered shirt. He was standing in what seemed to be his favourite position before the impressive rock fireplace, directing his remarks to the man seated with his back to her on the leather chair facing the patio doors. A woman, blonde and in her

late twenties, sat opposite him in a dress of blood red
that fitted closely the lines of a lushly provocative
figure.

Frowning, Lee walked quickly along the passage
to the stairs. She had had no experience of social
converse with a woman who practised what the new
morality preached. Already she herself felt colourless
in her pale sophistication.

Pausing for only a moment at the foot of the stairs,
she put a reassuring palm across the smooth drawback of her hair and ran her hands over the hips of a
dress that suggested the shape of her body beneath it
in tasteful fashion, yet which emphasised her femininity in its low neckline revealing the beginning
swell of her breasts. The sapphire blue of the dress
made a night-sky drama of her wide spaced eyes, and
pinpointed the jewels at her throat and wrist.

Without conceit, she knew that she looked her best.
She was unprepared, however, for the reactions from
the other members of the house party when at last she
stepped into their view. Kelsey looked up from the
glass he held loosely in his hand, an odd stillness
freezing him to immobility. The blonde woman
gaped openly for the space of a full minute before a
series of conflicting emotions darted across her
slightly hard brown eyes. Surprise, awe, envy.

'Well, go ahead,' the man with his back to her said
impatiently to Kelsey, his full head of black hair suspiciously shiny, 'let's hear the rest of it. Fishing's not
in my line, but I have to admit——'

As if sensing the presence that held the other two in
rock-like suspension, the sleek black head turned and

caught a glimpse of Lee.

'I'm sorry, am I late?' she apologised, moving farther into the room and hearing the sound of her own voice that fell with bell-like clarity into the yawning silence of the room.

'Late? My God, I'd wait for ever to catch sight of a woman like you!' Harry Vendisi told her, awestruck as he struggled with what she thought must be uncharacteristic gallantry to his feet. Dark circles lay like bruises under his dark Latin eyes, and Lee caught a glimpse of unhealthily pallid facial skin and the unfit bulges his dinner jacket did little to hide. His head swivelled accusingly back to Kelsey. 'I didn't know you had a wife like this hidden away, but——' his eyes went appreciatively back to Lee, 'I can sure understand why you'd want to hide her at that. She's beautiful.'

Feeling like a prime specimen on the auction block, Lee looked instinctively to Kelsey and he, sensing her embarrassment, came to stand by her side, his fingers warmly reassuring on her elbow as he introduced her.

'Unfortunately she's not my wife, Harry. This is Mrs Whitney—Lee.'

'*You're*——?' Vendisi's jaw dropped as he stared speechlessly at Lee.

'This is Harry Vendisi, Lee,' Kelsey went smoothly on, the pressure of his fingers on her waist light as he turned her in the blonde woman's direction. 'And this is Bobbi Schwartz, his—companion on the trip.'

Lee suppressed a sharp inclination to giggle disbelievingly; it was all too much like a Grade B movie!

Gangster and moll, Harry and Bobbi! All the scene needed was two burly bodyguards to make it truly authentic. Bobbi patted the vacant sofa seat beside her and Lee left the inexplicable comfort of Kelsey's sheltering arm to move across to the frankly apprais- ing other woman.

'Are you for real?' Bobbi enquired with some of the awe Vendisi, now re-seated but still regarding her with disbelieving eyes, had exhibited moments before. 'I mean—you're *really* Mrs Whitney, the big tycoon from Frisco?'

Realising that whatever she answered would sound like an affirmation of greatness, Lee murmured that she headed Whitney Enterprises, but that 'I have some very astute people I rely on.'

'Men?'

'Yes.'

'For a minute,' Vendisi chuckled, seeming oddly relieved, 'I thought you were one of those women who tries to go it alone in the big bad world of busi- ness.' The limpid dark eyes shaded slightly to hard- ness. 'I hope you brought one of your whiz-kids with you. I don't have too much time to——'

'To deal with a woman?' Lee interposed sweetly, her mouth widening to an artless smile. 'As a matter of fact, Mr Vendisi, I came alone. You see, I happen to make the major decisions for Whitney, based on my own calculations of profit and loss to the company of any new investment. Based, of course,' she smiled her relaxed thanks for the drink Kelsey handed to her, surprising approval in his black eyes as they met hers briefly, 'on the background research my assistants very ably provide. For instance,' she sipped slowly from her glass, her eyes obscured by the darkened fan of her lashes until she looked swiftly, disconcertingly, into the shocked brown of Vendisi's, 'it was brought to my attention that Vendar Shipping did a high average of business until last year, when it fell off considerably.'

'That was only because of inflation,' Vendisi blustered defensively, lost between his admiration for a beautiful woman and the knowledge that he was facing a formidable business mind. The two so obviously confused his thinking that Kelsey intervened smoothly.

'Inflation is something we've all got to deal with, but tonight,' he smiled, deliberately relaxed, 'we're going to forget business and enjoy an evening in each other's company.' Following his own philosophy, he turned companionably to the still shaken Vendisi. 'I know you've said you're not interested in fishing, Harry, but I think I might change your mind if you come out with me on the boat. I can almost guarantee a fine salmon.'

Deftly, he relaxed the atmosphere until even Vendisi seemed to forget his qualms about a competent woman of business and Lee, forgetting the ire the older man had roused by his chauvinistic attitude, found herself caught up in Kelsey's enthusiasm for the unfamiliar world beyond business and left her wishing, as dinner drew to a close, that she too could be involved in the fighting submission of a coho on the line.

'Maybe you and Bobbi can amuse yourself around

the pool for the day,' Kelsey suggested, scotching that idea. Not that she would have gone fishing anyway. The rugged world of the outdoors had never been her scene, and her imagination boggled at the thought of the curvy Bobbi baiting a hook with her extra long blood-red nails. The prospect of a whole day indulging female chatter round the pool was no less ludicrous.

'That's more in my line,' Bobbi looked up brightly from the delicately risen soufflé she was toying with, her brown eyes going appraisingly over Lee's pale skin. 'You could do with a little tan, too,' she criticised.

'I don't have much time to sunbathe,' Lee retorted coolly, emphasising without meaning to her own busily packed life in comparison with Bobbi's. 'My skin burns very easily, anyway,' she hastened to add.

'Oh, I know,' Bobbi commiserated, 'my skin's the same. But you know, if you do it gradually——'

Lee scarcely listened as the other woman launched into a diatribe on the advantages of acquiring a gradual suntan. What a bore the next few days were going to be! Maybe she could speed up the business aspect of their visit and cut short her stay on the island. She was as far from her goal of extracting revenge on Kelsey as she had ever been anyway.

After dinner, they all adjourned to the lower level of the house, where Kelsey and Harry proposed a pool championship. Slightly behind the other two as they descended to the basement games room, Lee was incensed when Kelsey slid an arm round her slenderly curved waist and pulled her to him so that she felt the tensed muscles in his thigh, the rigidly controlled pleasantness in his voice.

'Just cool the efficient business woman image, will you?' he breathed softly at her ear. 'Harry's not the type to take kindly to gimlet-eyed women who wear corporate pants.'

'That's just too bad,' she whispered back. 'I don't happen to subscribe to his medieval thinking that skirts belong only in the kitchen providing for the needs of man!'

Before Kelsey had time to formulate a reply she had pulled away, joining Bobbi on the spectator chairs set back from the green baize of the pool table.

Random thoughts swooped down and momentarily captured her attention, diffusing her interest in the game. Was Kelsey really as anxious to acquire Harry's shipping line as he seemed? Just how much did the Roberts Corporation need the added revenues another company's assets would bring it? The information collated by her marketing staff had been startlingly inconclusive. The Roberts brothers were doing adquately; they were solvent, owing nothing to anyone. But Kelsey, being Kelsey, wouldn't be satisfied with an average score. Years ago, with very few funds at his disposal, he stabbed at gaining control of Whitney's Frantug operation. He was a man of wide vision, driving ambition, she acknowledged sourly, letting her reluctant eyes linger on his smooth-muscled figure as it bent lithely over the velvet green of the pool table. He needed her to close a deal with Harry; and in view of Harry's very obvious distaste for women in powerful positions, it seemed that she in turn needed him.

Bobbi's despairing, 'Oh, Harry, what in the world are you doing?' brought Lee's attention back to the game unfolding before them. The vari-coloured balls ricocheted on the background of green, careening wildly on its velvet surface with none of them disappearing into the holes placed at intervals round the table. She looked at Bobbi, half envious of her obvious knowledge of the game. What made a woman live the kind of life she did, even now subsiding quickly back into her seat as Harry Vendisi glared at her vindictively.

'You think you can do it better?' he demanded ferociously, and Bobbi half disappeared into the chair.

'No, of course I can't, Harry. I—I was just encouraging you, that's all.'

His flat eyes blistered her. 'With encouragement like that, who needs a friend to pull him down?' he snarled with rhetorical bitterness. His head swivelled back to the table and the dark shadows under his eyes seemed to deepen even further as he watched Kelsey's steady-handed manipulation of the cue. His mouth tightened to a tightly pursed line, and Lee presumed that Kelsey's shot had been good.

Unexpectedly, she found herself silently tense on Kelsey's behalf. She knew nothing about the game, but Harry's increasingly flustered expression told her that he was losing, and badly. It seemed an unfair competition, she thought with vagrant humour, her eyes making swift inspection of Harry's unfit bulges before going on more lingeringly to Kelsey's streamlined contours, shoulder muscles moving in a controlled rhythm as he lined up the ball again. Ridicul-

ously, she wanted to run her hands through the black
thickness of his hair, to feel its vibrant texture between her fingers. Or was it so ridiculous? He was the
only man she had been that close to; her sensitive
nerve ends remembered the feel of that vigorous
growth, its cool thickness ... involuntarily, the
thought of Maitland crossed her mind, and she
almost giggled aloud at the thought of running her
fingers through his hair. Such a gesture would have
caused acute embarrassment on his part and a distaste for his carefully arranged fair strands on hers.

'I'll play you a re-match,' Harry was saying trucu-
lently to a coolly triumphant Kelsey, who glanced at
the two women sitting side by side beyond the down-
ward-slanting lights over the pool table.

'I think the ladies have had enough for one night's
viewing,' he suggested, his eyes slanting an obscure
message to Lee, one she took up immediately but
which she didn't fully understand. Obviously Kelsey
wanted her to agree with him, to make known her
disenchantment with the basement games room, but
why that should be she had no idea. However, she rose
and said tactfully to the perspiring Harry,

'I don't pretend to know the first thing about pool,
but I can guess I've seen a match between two pros.'

Hesitating only slightly, Harry walked across to
replace his cue in the board. 'It's been some time
since I played,' he excused himself, not looking at the
quiet Bobbi as he crossed to Lee and took her arm
possessively. 'But before I leave this tarnation island
I'll beat that son of a gun.'

'Of course you will, Harry.' Bobbi rose and came

to slide an intimate arm into the crook of Harry's, a vindictive hatred flashing quickly over her inanimate features as he moved off with Lee towards the stairs, her arm dropping uselessly at her side.

Hatred ... for herself, or for the man she had attached herself to? Lee wondered as she followed the pressure on her arm. Yet why would Bobbi stay with Harry, following him around like a love starved puppy, when he treated her so offhandedly? Poor Bobbi, life must have dealt her some hard blows for her to accept, now, the sporadic favours of an unattractive type like Harry Vendisi.

Back upstairs in the spacious living room, she detached her arm from Harry's restraining fingers and said, 'If you'll excuse me, I think I'll get to bed now.' Her eyes, shaded to deep violet blue, automatically sought Kelsey's. 'It's been quite a day.' If she had expected an outer manifestation that Kelsey, as much as she, remembered that fraught scene in her bathroom there was no sign of it as he said easily, crossing to the bar,

'Nonsense. Let's have a drink before we call it a day.' Asking no one's preference, he poured generous measures of brandy into balloon glasses and carried them in turn to Lee, Bobbi, and finally to the still disgruntled Harry. 'Here's to our re-match.'

'Yeah.' Harry almost snatched the expensive crystal from his hand and tossed the brandy back in one large-sized swallow. Unaffected, he went on as he placed the glass on the square coffee table. 'We'll have another game tomorrow, and we'll see then who's the best man.' Nodding imperiously at the wide-eyed Bobbi, he said curtly, 'Let's go.'

Placing her untouched glass beside his on the table, she accompanied him docilely to the stairs which were out of view of the living room. 'Goodnight,' she smiled fleetingly to Lee and Kelsey, then trotted obediently after the stocky figure who was apparently her lord and master. Irritated, Lee set down her similarly untouched drink and said waspishly to the immobile Kelsey,

'Doesn't she have a mind of her own? Does she have to move like a puppet when he pulls the strings?'

Kelsey moved then, his arm lifting the glass to his mouth before he looked at Lee with what might have been a glint of humour.

'Maybe she likes a macho type man, maybe she's in love with him, who knows?' He moved closer, so that Lee was forced to acknowledge his nearness. 'Some women do like to feel there's a man in charge. But that wouldn't be you, would it, Lee?'

Her own violent reaction to the touch of his fingers on the white skin of her upper arm shocked even herself. Yet she was powerless to pull away; part of her wanted to, knew she must, but the clamouring insistence of deprived nerve ends left her paralysed, bereft of the control she had exercised over her senses since a night seven years before. A night when every moral precept she had absorbed from a loving upbringing had fled like so many straws in the wind. The outer layers of her being rejected the strong pull of her senses, yet she was helpless against the forceful undercurrent that seemed to run between his skin and hers, sending the pulsing beat of sensual awareness into every atom of her being. She tried to speak, but her voice was lost in an emotional upsurge that left her gasping.

'Kelsey, I——'

What had she wanted to say, to tell him? Inexplicably, nothing seemed important except the insistent rise of her heartbeat against the thrusting power of his. Nothing seemed to surprise her. Her lips should be firming, tightening, against the nearness of his, yet they softened, opened, to his touch, welcoming the abrasive touch of his male chin, the lean bow of his body as his hands moulded the soft curve of her hips to his.

'Lee...' he murmured at her ear, repeating the anguished words against the erratic pulse at her throat, making her head jerk back in an access of naked longing that made nonsense of the years between. Her need was open, as high pitched as Kelsey's male-orientated desire. Her fingers touched and held to the smooth line of his shoulders and she moaned as they at last tangled in the vibrant growth of his hair, the black hair which she knew was repeated on the wide expanse of his chest.

'God, Lee, I love you,' he moaned when her fingertips ran sensitively over the outer shell of his ears before plunging back into the rampant growth of his hair. 'And I want you—stay with me tonight, Lee, it's been so long.'

So long... yes, so very long since she had heard this singing in her veins, this need that battered against her defences and left them wanting...

So long... the words echoed in her mind as Kelsey

stooped to lift her into his arms against him, weaving a discordant thread as he mounted the red-carpeted stairs to the upper floor. It was as if ... as if he remembered that grinding need she had fought so hard to overcome. But that couldn't be ... all he had meant was that it had been so long since he had made love to a woman. Any woman. His wife had died a short year before, the wife who had laid claim to him even as Lee had woven her girlish dreams around him ...

It was the remembrance of his wife that cut a clear patch in the fogginess of her mind. Kelsey was incapable of fidelity to one woman—who knew that better than herself? Any long-term commitment, which was all that would satisfy her, was alien to his nature. Kelsey could never be faithful to her or any woman.

Thought was parent to action. When Kelsey paused at her door, one hand groping for the handle, Lee loosed her hold on his neck and swung her feet to the floor, contrarily missing the warmth of Kelsey's body as hers moved to the door he had swung open. Grasping the handle and turning from there, she looked levelly into his eyes, already beginning to smoulder.

'Thanks for an interesting evening,' she said in a voice unmistakably dismissing. A dark flush rose under his tanned skin as he stepped forcefully towards her.

'What in hell is this? Another brush-off?'

'If you care to call it that. I'm just not available for casual encounters, Kelsey, they're not my thing.'

'That wasn't what you thought a few minutes ago

down there!' His hand curled round hers and brought her to the heated line of his body. Triumph gleamed briefly at the back of his eyes when she drew a deep, denying breath. 'What in God's name is your price for sharing your bed—*marriage*?'

Sickness churned within her, but she managed a sweet, 'I'm old-fashioned that way.' With a deft movement, murmuring goodnight at the same time, she entered her room and closed the door firmly in his face.

There was no lock on the door and she leaned back on it for long fraught moments until some sixth sense reassured her that Kelsey had departed noiselessly on the thick hall carpeting to his own room. But two more minutes ticked by while she guarded the door like a Vestal Virgin defending her chastity. Then, her limbs stiff, she walked to the dressing table and stared dispassionately at her reflection in the mirror there. Her cheeks were flushed to delicate rose which in turn sparked stars in her eyes. Starry-eyed! Turning away in disgust, she reached for the low back zipper on her dress.

She wasn't a starry-eyed teenager any more, expecting the conventional outcome when two people loved emotionally, desired physically ... what she felt for Kelsey was purely on that physical basis. Gingham curtains at a cottage window were as alien to him as a tract house would be to a hardnosed millionaire businessman.

Which Kelsey was, she told herself in the elegantly appointed bathroom as she creamed make-up from her face. He was the perfect example of the 'now' generation, which made no bones about indulging the passing passions that were meant to last only on a short-term basis. Scrubbing her evenly spaced teeth with automatic strokes, Lee rejected the thinking of Kelsey and others like him. How could there be any permanence, any deeply satisfying relationship, when neither partner knew which drifting wind might bear the other way?

Straight and still under the covers, the curtains drawn back to allow the flood of a harvest type moon to illuminate the room, Lee conjured up a picture of what her life with Maitland would be. Unexciting, perhaps, but stable, secure in a way she would never know with a man like Kelsey. Her thinking faltered ... would her body crave, at its deepest centre, the unsatisfied longing it now battled with? Could Maitland inspire the floating dream of ecstasy Kelsey brought to life with the merest touch of his sunbronzed hand?

She turned restlessly, her eyes catching the glint of moonlight from the adjoining sitting room. Why hadn't Kelsey's wife liked the island? Surely, if she had loved Kelsey it would have been a peaceful oasis, a haven for two people who loved each other. Love! Why was it so important? Wasn't a civilised regard a better basis for lifelong commitment? The kind she and Maitland had for each other. No ecstatic highs, perhaps, but no despondent lows either. A calm, serene, ordered existence ... she would have that with Maitland, not the grinding, all-pervasive need men like Kelsey inspired. ...

*

The morning was foggy, of the kind Lee was familiar with in San Francisco. The curling white wisps winding around the tree tops would soon disperse, but the other two guests on Madrona Island were of a different mind.

'You're crazy,' Harry stated flatly at breakfast in the small sitting room, addressing an aggressively fit Kelsey whose tan was emphasised by the whiteness of his casual shirt tucked into tailored blue denims. 'There's no way I'd go out in that kind of weather.'

'By the time we're ready to go,' Kelsey returned, amusement under his steady tone, 'the fog will have lifted. There's a run of coho around the islands right now, so we should be able to catch tonight's dinner at least.'

'I don't like fish much,' Bobbi, conversely dressed in blue sailor-striped top and white sail pants, threw into the conversation plaintively.

'You might like it more if you have a hand in catching it,' Kelsey said with a soft indulgence in his voice, and Lee looked sharply up from her grapefruit half. Surely he wouldn't be so stupid as to—her eyes flicked to Bobbi's generous curves outlined under the clinging top. There was an innocent freshness about her, combined with an unconscious sexiness that would appeal to a man like Kelsey. The thought was enough for Lee to set down her spoon beside the half-finished grapefruit, her appetite soured. Why had she let herself in for this kind of hassle after being free from the destructive emotion of jealousy for so many years? Was jealousy the right word? She had had her chance of becoming Kelsey's lover more than once during this trip; a lover in the no-strings-attached way Kelsey excelled in. Maybe she felt pity for the vulnerable Bobbi, who was apparently content to stay in the background of Harry Vendisi's life, expecting no more from the relationship than her board and lodging. Impatience tinged her sympathy. Was it really necessary, in this day and age, for a woman to accept the gratuitous offerings of a man of Vendisi's calibre?

She became aware of three pairs of eyes looking appraisingly at her and a flush ran under her cheeks as she looked instinctively to Kelsey, so firmly in command at the head of the table, the amused glint in his dark eyes telling her that he had spoken to her more than once.

'I'm sorry, did you say something?'

'I said I think you should come with us too. It's quite an experience to catch your first salmon.'

Lee's brows rose frigidly. No 'Would you care to come?' Just his decision that she should accompany them on the fishing trip. 'No, thanks, it's not something that appeals to me.'

'How do you know until you try it?' Kelsey countered drily, and logically. It almost seemed as if he really wanted her to go—perhaps to prove that his prowess in catching fish was greater than Harry's, his inflated male ego wanting to score in her eyes. It would be a shame to miss his chagrin if the fish opted for Harry's bait rather than his. Besides, an empty day alone with Bobbi on Madrona Island appealed to her even less than a day on a fishing boat.

'All right, I'll come.' She accepted with an acknowledging smile the lightly boiled egg and crisp buttered toast that Freda placed before her, then looked at Kelsey, who hadn't taken his eyes off her. 'Where do you keep your fishing boat?' she asked casually. 'I haven't seen one at the jetty.'

Amusement gleamed momentarily in his dark eyes, as if he suspected that she had given thought to leaving the island independently.

'I keep it at the far side of the island. It's closer to the best fishing grounds there.'

She would never have found it, she reflected half an hour later as she followed Kelsey's free springing stride along a wending forest path that led down to an idyllic small cove, Harry and the reluctant Bobbi arguing volubly behind her, the beauty of their surroundings lost on them.

And it was beautiful. Private, quiet, protectively treed to the small half circle sandy beach. A boathouse of cedar blended into the rustic landscape, and at the short dock a vessel about twice the size of the cabin cruiser rocked gently at anchor.

'Like it?'

Hardly realising she had halted, Lee stared blankly at Kelsey, who had turned back on the downward path. Walking faster than the other two, whose quarrelsome voices came only distantly now, it seemed she and Kelsey alone shared the cove's beauty, its serenity.

Her voice seemed uncharacteristically breathless as she said, simply, 'Yes. It's beautiful.'

'I guessed you would like it. And you'll enjoy fishing too, I can promise you that.'

He seemed eager, even boyishly anxious to please her and be pleased himself at her appreciation of the island he obviously loved. The moment of communion splintered as the other two panted up heavily behind them, Harry calling out irascibly,

'How much farther is it to this boat of yours, Kelsey? I wish you'd told us we were going on a wildlife hike, Bobbi's fallen over tree roots a million times since we left the house!'

'As you'll see,' Kelsey retorted drily, turning back to resume his downward trek to the cove, 'we're almost there.'

Lee let the perspiring pair pass her, noting as they went Bobbi's totally unsuitable open-toed heeled sandals. No wonder she had stumbled over the numerous tree roots edging their way across the pine-needled path.

Her mind was so totally immersed in her inner cogitations that her own feet, in thick-soled runners, stubbed painfully against the treacherous taproots liberally sprinkled along the downward path. Could Kelsey's marriage have been all that happy when his wife had shared none of his pleasure in this island which meant so much to him? When faithfulness took a back seat to sexual indulgence on Kelsey's business trips? When he felt free to seduce the inexperienced teenager she had been? And how many others had succumbed to his total male charm? Disgust for the woman Kelsey had married flooded acridly into her throat as Lee reached the flat land leading to the tiny pier. If she had made him happy, complete, he would have felt no need to seduce innocent girls who fell for his practised charms.

Was she making excuses for him?

She paused at the entrance to the wood-slatted pier, which swayed slightly under the combined weight of the three who had gone ahead. The realisation that she *did* want to make excuses came like a body blow that fanned out inside her and spread golden warmth through her limbs. Like a lake breaking up from an ice-bound winter she felt herself come alive in a way she had never thought would be possible again.

Her hand trembled and groped for the roughly hewn rail bordering the pier. She couldn't love Kelsey still; none of her life for the past seven years made sense if she did. With or without a wife he had the low-grade morals of an alley cat. Every fibre in her knew that she didn't welcome this pulsing glow that was permeating every part of her being, but— even the sight of Kelsey's lithe leap on to the fishing vessel had the power to send hurtful surges of longing through her, a renewal of the feelings she had thrust out of existence long ago. Her mind was numb while her body remembered the feel of his naked skin on hers, the consuming mastery of his practised lips and hands, the indescribable satisfaction in his possession.

She clung weakly to the rail, lost in the deep depression of her thoughts until Kelsey's voice penetrated her consciousness.

'What's wrong? Do boats scare you?'

She blinked at him dazedly, sensing somehow that it was important to him that she didn't disappoint him by proving a bad sailor. 'I—no, boats don't bother me. I just—wanted to get my bearings, that's all.'

'Oh.'

The one word spoke volumes and Lee, remembering his almost psychic ability to sense her thoughts, mustered the remnants of her cool personality.

'Shall we go, then? Bobbi looks seasick already.'

Her eyes followed the swivel of his head back to where Bobbi, her face pale, clutched the boat-rail with white-knuckled fingers. Her attention was far from the nervous Bobbi, however. Her eyes took in with the newness of discovery the strength of Kelsey's profile, the deep set of his dark eyes with their firmly marked black brows, the not quite perfect straightness of his nose, the firm set of his lips, the strong thrust of his dark-shaded chin. She loved him, she thought dispassionately; against all sense and reason, she loved him from the thick sweep of his black hair to the feet covered in rubber-soled deck shoes. But he was the last person in the world who would have that information, she told herself firmly, steeling herself against the light touch of his fingers on her bare elbow as he urged her along the wooden pier.

'It's up to Harry to take care of Bobbi,' he said with callous indifference. 'I'm not at my best with seasick landlubbers.'

But his actions seemed to deny those words when the expedition was under way. Lee even spared a wry inner smile for her own worries about him discovering her new knowledge, for Kelsey spent a large part of the trip with Bobbi, showing her how to hold the rod he cajoled into her white manicured hands, laughing at her little-girl squeals of delight when a small salmon hooked on to her lure. Harry was occupied with his own rod on the far side of the boat, so it was Kelsey who, his arms circling the voluptuous curves of Bobbi's superbly female figure, helped her land the three-pound fish.

As Bobbi turned her ecstatic features up to Kelsey's, her seasickness evidently forgotten, Lee turned back to watch her own rod, unquivering as the boat trolled slowly within easy sight of land. How she would love to bring to heel a massive salmon that would make Kelsey's eyes bulge with envy! She had watched carefully how he had manipulated Bobbi's fish, and knew she could handle one much bigger.

She stared as the rod assigned to her bent suddenly towards the water; it was as if the gods had heard her earnest plea for supremacy.

'Probably just some seaweed,' Kelsey said laconically from behind her shoulder as she lifted the rod from its holder and began to reel in. She paused.

'Seaweed?' she enquired indignantly. 'Why should you think that?'

'Because the pull on the tip is fairly regular,' he responded in a voice so filled with amusement that she wanted to hit him—and Bobbi—and even the temporarily absorbed Harry Vendisi. 'When it's a fish, the rod tip bends erratically and your line zings out from the reel.' Amusement changed to enthusiasm. 'There's nothing in the world like the sound of a reel being pulled by a fighting salmon.'

There was chagrin in Lee's disgusted appraisal of the hook emerging from the ocean depths dripping heavy, dark green seaweed. Although Kelsey cleared the line with cheerful disregard, humiliation seethed just under Lee's outwardly disdainful surface. The inane Bobbi had managed to capture a fish, however small; why couldn't she?

She thanked Kelsey frigidly as he returned her rod to its holder, and her coolness evidently got through to him because his eyes seemed to flicker far back in their midnight depths before he stood back and watched the even flow of her line through the water.

'I can manage now, thanks,' she said coolly, and with a briefly appraising look, he withdrew to the far side of the boat where his own line awaited his attention.

Irritably, Lee focused her eyes on the regular flexing of her rod tip, angry because her traitorous body missed his vital presence. There was nothing about the symmetric rise and fall of the sensitive rod tip to preclude the alien thoughts clustering into her mind. If they were alone on the boat, without even the presence of Freda's stoically inclined husband at the bridge, what would they be doing now? Guarding the tensile rods, or focusing their attention on each other? That last possibility spawned a dreamlike state where, as in a slow moving film, she saw Kelsey's tanned body lowering over the milk whiteness of her own, his lips persuasive as they traced the trembling fullness of hers, the warm surrender of her flesh to the male demands of his. . . .

A loud zing on her line sent those errant thoughts scuttling on their way to oblivion. Panicked, she stared at the violently vibrating tip of her rod, knowing that a fish of some sort had succumbed to the desire for her lure. What did she do now?

'Kelsey,' she called, then louder, 'Kelsey!'

He was there behind her as if he had been waiting for her call, his bronzed forearms stiff against her ribs as they circled her and detached the rod from its holder.

'It's a big one, Lee,' he exulted, muscles straining as he raised the rod into the air and brought it down to the level of her nerveless arms. 'Take it,' he said urgently, 'feel how he's running!'

'You do it.' Lee succumbed to the panic running high in her bloodstream and dropped her hands from the cushioned cork of the rod handle, only to find them forced back to a hold reinforced by Kelsey's leanly competent fingers.

'Do it yourself,' he commanded briefly, but his hands seemed reluctant to release their warm hold over hers. She felt the length of his hard body behind her as he guided her manipulation of the rod, its screeching ratchet as the fish fought for freedom punctuating her awareness of his muscled thighs, stomach, chest pressing intimately close to her own contours.

The fish, glinting silver in the sunlight, made a tremendous leap in the water an incredible distance away. Lee instinctively began to reel in, the ratchet stiff and flexible by turns as she played the fish until at last it was exhaustedly near the boat side. Moments later, it lay quivering on the bleached boards of the fishing boat, its size incredible to her inexperienced eyes.

'No, don't!' she cried out as Kelsey raised a spiked gaff to club it to death, but it was too late. The fish lay immobile on the weathered boards, its life extinguished by the skilful blow Kelsey directed.

'Fantastic, Lee!' he exulted, turning back with glowing eyes to grip her briefly to him, excitement of the moment lighting the deep centres of his eyes to a contagious glow. 'It must weigh over ten pounds!'

Pride of capturing a prize so obviously desirable in Kelsey's eyes disposed of the major parts of her distaste for the horror of it all, but Lee still felt slightly sick as Bobbi and Harry, attracted by Kelsey's exultant shouts, circled round the inanimate prize catch.

'Well, I guess you've won the day's stakes,' Harry said with reluctant admiration, his eyes fixed on the slenderly formed fish glistening its silver-lined underbelly on the boards. 'Guess we might as well make for home now.'

'Good idea,' Kelsey surprisingly approved, turning his head towards the wheelhouse. 'Let's take her in, Bill.'

While he attended to the fish Lee leaned with her back to the rail and Harry glanced down sourly at her catch as he sauntered towards her.

'Are you always this lucky first time around?' he asked, half curious, half sneering.

'I never rely on luck where business is concerned,' Lee returned crisply, 'and so far that's been my main interest.' Distastefully, she switched her gaze from his muddy brown eyes and looked over to where Kelsey was extracting hooks from the fish's mouth, his fingers long and supple like the rest of him. Her mental comparison between the two men was far from flattering to Harry Vendisi.

'Kelsey here seems to think you run your company single-handed,' he said snidely, his eyes going crudely down over the pointed thrust of her breasts, narrow hips and elegant length of leg. 'I find that hard to believe. There's no way you can tell me a good-looking woman like you doesn't have at least one man to take care of things for her.'

Lee appraised him coolly. 'All right, I won't try to tell you. It would be a waste of time, wouldn't it? You can't tell a man who's living in the past anything.'

'What do you mean by that?' he blustered, suddenly looking ugly and bringing to Lee's mind all the horrendous stories she had heard about mob violence. It wouldn't be hard to imagine Harry Vendisi putting the kiss of death on anyone who crossed him.

'Just what I said,' she told him with a calmness that surprised even herself. 'You're living in the long past days when women did no more than darn their husbands' socks and cook his meals.'

'You forgot keeping his bed warm,' he leered with the arrogance of a man who kept a woman like Bobbi for his personal satisfactions. 'Or are you also one of those women who doesn't need a man around?'

'I think Lee's personal life is her own affair,' Kelsey's voice, quietly even, came from behind him. 'I asked her to come here and discuss business, and as far as I'm concerned that's all she has to do while she's at Madrona Island.'

Whether Harry sensed the veiled threat underlying Kelsey's words or if he had become bored with Lee and what she stood for, he backed down with unusual grace.

'All right, I apologise. I'm just not used to the idea of doing business with a woman. But now that I know, let's get it over as soon as we can.'

'Whenever you're ready,' Kelsey agreed levelly. 'We can start talking tonight after dinner if you want.'

'That's fine.' With those staccato words, Harry stomped off to where Bobbi had stretched out on the afterdeck to sun herself. Kelsey turned back to Lee, a strange light at the back of his eyes.

'Sorry about that,' he bit off curtly. 'If you want to call the whole thing off, it's all right by me.'

'Call it off?' Lee echoed, staring directly into his eyes perplexedly. 'I thought this deal was important to you?'

He shrugged, and half turned away. 'We'll survive.'

'We haven't discussed Frantug yet,' Lee reminded him softly, and his eyes swivelled back to hers as if he understood what she was saying underneath. If the Vendisi deal fell through, there was still the possibility of expansion for the Roberts Company, his and his brother's.

'No, we haven't, have we?' he said thoughtfully, but somehow Lee had the impression that business was far from his mind at that moment. . . .

CHAPTER SIX

THERE was a strained silence between the four as they retraced their steps through the forest area to the comfortably set house overlooking the bay. Even Bobbi seemed subdued, making no complaint even when, as happened often, she stubbed her uncovered toes on half-hidden projections along the winding path.

Lee was too conscious of Kelsey's unhurried pace behind her to conjecture much on what had transpired on the boat. All that came and went in her mind was the knowledge that she had more or less pledged the Frantug operation to him. What had possessed her? The whole idea of this trip to his home ground had been to thwart every business move he made ... yet she had virtually handed Frantug to him on a platter. She felt strangely hollow inside, as if the bitterness she had known for years had gone and left nothing to replace it.

Could love do that to people? To a woman respected in business circles for her hard-headed acumen? Of course not! She had simply been reacting to Harry Vendisi's crude assessment of woman's place being at her man's side, a little behind his arrogant stride.

They entered the house by the sliding door into the living room, and it took Lee several seconds to adjust to the dimmer light after the sunshine outside. She saw the shapes of two hazy figures rise from the fire-side area, heard Kelsey's muffled oath as he recognised them.

'Well, Kelsey,' a woman's tart voice reached them, waking violent memories in Lee, 'we've been waiting since noon for you to get back.'

Ignoring the censure in her voice, Kelsey said from just behind Lee's shoulder, 'If I'd known you and Phil were coming, Dorothy, I'd have made arrangements for you to be met.'

'We just decided at the last minute to come over, and I really think you should replace that stupid boy you've left in charge of the boat. He refused to bring us over at first,' she reported indignantly, 'and then when I said that we own the island——'

'A very small part of it,' Kelsey reminded her with quiet irony, but he went forward to greet his sister-in-law with a perfunctory kiss. 'Geoff's been given instructions that no unauthorised visitors are to be brought over to Madrona. He's never seen you before, so it's only natural——'

'He was very rude about it,' Dorothy interrupted as if used to having her word unquestioned, and she looked round at the island's guests while Kelsey went to shake the hand of a younger edition of himself.

Younger, Lee thought involuntarily, and infinitely weaker in physique and, she suspected, character. But other thoughts were uppermost in her mind as Dorothy's gimlet eyes lit on herself and stared penetratingly. Oh, God, would she remember the girl Kelsey had shared his room with in San Francisco those years ago? Unlike Kelsey, her memory had not been obscured by the accident that had taken his wife's life.

'*You!*' those flat clouded eyes seemed to say, but Dorothy smiled without recognition when Kelsey drew Lee forward and introduced her just moments before Harry, unused to taking a place in the background, stepped forward with Bobbi in tow.

'Oh, Mr Vendisi,' she gushed, 'I'm so happy to meet you. I—that is, *Phil* and I,' she amended belatedly, 'have heard so much about you, and——'

'You have?' Harry's frown brought an immediate about-face from Dorothy.

'Only from Kelsey, of course,' she said nervously, looking not at her husband but at Kelsey's tautly withdrawn expression. 'It's so exciting to think that we might be taking over *your* business in Seattle,' she prattled on. 'Our company has been expanding so rapidly that I find it hard to keep up.'

'I'm sure that's not true,' Harry returned gallantly, if a little drily, his eyes shifting to where Phil Roberts, his slender body dwarfed by his brother's, stood uncertainly beside Kelsey.

'It's by no means sure that the Whitney Company, in co-operation with the Roberts Company, will be interested in what Mr Vendisi has to offer,' Lee inserted smoothly, wanting to hustle the garrulous Dorothy out of the room before she could sabotage any bargaining strongpoints she and Kelsey might have. 'We've come here to throw around a few ideas, and see if we can come up with a deal acceptable to all concerned.'

'And our first round of talks is taking place after dinner tonight,' Kelsey inserted smoothly, his eyes flicking a brief approval in Lee's direction. 'But first, we'll all have dinner together.' He cocked an enquiring eye at Lee. 'Do you think your fish will run to dinner for six?'

'I think it might,' she smiled back at him, mainly in relief, and saw Dorothy's suspicious gaze dart rapidly between them.

'I don't think you've met my brother yet,' Kelsey offered, stretching out a hand towards Lee, who ignored Dorothy's inquisitive look and went forward to clasp the smooth warmth of his spare flesh, conscious of his continued clasp as he introduced the brother who was so like, yet unlike, himself.

'It's a pleasure to meet you, Mrs Whitney.'

There was even a resemblance in the voice, but without Kelsey's underlying forcefulness. A wave of what could only be maternal protectiveness swept over her as she looked into eyes that were dark like Kelsey's yet with a softer patina to them. For the first time, the name Fletcher had bestowed on her had a false ring to it.

The thought followed her up to her room a few minutes later, and into the bathroom where she took a leisurely bath to iron out the wrinkles the day's unusual exercise had crimped into her muscles.

She had loved Fletcher, of course, as a daughter loves an indulgent father, as a niece loves a doting uncle. But the feelings she had known for Fletcher were bland, soft, undemanding compared to the violent response every part of her felt, welcomed, when

Kelsey touched her, however lightly. She was a child again then, with all of a child's wonder at the new sensations flooding her, and yet she felt herself a woman with a woman's response to a loved male's demands.

A man, she reminded herself as she stepped from the soapy tub and towelled herself briskly, who was incapable of a woman's quality of love, who lived and loved without thought for tomorrow. But that wasn't enough for her.

Her hands slowed and grew still on the thirsty thickness of the towel as she stared unseeingly ahead. She wanted, needed, the security of a love without fear, without doubts. And she would never have that with Kelsey.

She had drawn on the silk folds of her long white dressing gown and let down her hair before the dressing table mirror when there was a slight tap on the door. The tumbled red-gold skeins swirled around her face as she swung her head questioningly to the door that was thrust open without invitation.

'Did you want something, Mrs Roberts?' she asked coolly of the falsely smiling Dorothy, who took the words as an invitation and came farther into the room, closing the door firmly behind her.

'I came to ask you just that,' she said with coy friendliness. 'I suppose you could call me the lady of the house since Su—Kelsey's wife is no longer here.'

Lee's brows rose fractionally. 'I understood she never was here—on the island, I mean.'

'Well, no, she didn't care for island living.' Dorothy sauntered across to the wide closet and made an appraising inspection of Lee's wardrobe. 'She was full of life herself, she couldn't bear the solitude in such an isolated spot. Poor dear, it's a mercy she was killed outright in the accident, she'd never have wanted to be tied to a wheelchair or anything like that.'

Would anyone? Lee wondered drily, silently.

'She was very beautiful, you know,' Dorothy went on, transferring her interest to the few but expensive jars of the creams and make-up Lee used. 'Kelsey just adored her—well, all men did—that's why he'll never forgive himself for what happened. That he was the cause of her death, I mean.'

Lee's fingers trembled slightly as she took up her brush and began to stroke the unruly mass of hair. 'You seem to have been very fond of her.'

Dorothy's throaty laugh grated on her ears. 'Well, of course I was, she was my cousin. And we were very close, although she was a few years younger, mainly because my parents brought her up after her own were killed when she was ten. Strange,' she mused, abandoning the dresser to go over to where Lee herself often stood, looking out at the dusk-edged view, 'that she should be killed in almost the same way as her parents were. Thank God she couldn't have known anything about it—she was killed outright. She used to dread that kind of death.'

Uncomfortable with so much talk of killing and death, Lee stared fixedly at her own reflection in the wide mirror. She looked more vulnerable than usual with her hair loose, and her mouth had a softer, fuller outline than it had had that morning, surely? Deep in her eyes there was a glow she hadn't noticed before.

Did love do that to people? It was flattering, she conceded absently, knowing that she hadn't looked this way for years. Not since. . . .

Dorothy was speaking again, her voice grown sharp and pointed. 'Kelsey won't marry again, Mrs Whitney. Oh, he has his needs like any other man, and he's never stinted himself when it comes to female companionship, but it can never come to anything.'

'You seem to be warning me, Mrs Roberts,' Lee swung round to face the older woman, her hair-brushing made futile by the lift and swirl of her gold tresses. Dorothy had turned from the window, too, and doubting recognition flushed her sallow cheeks.

'My God, it can't be,' she breathed, the feverish glint in her eyes going over the mass of hair and white skin exposed by the fallen open front of Lee's robe. 'You're—that girl? The one in—San Francisco?'

Lee straightened and looked calmly at her. What did it matter that Dorothy Roberts recognised her as that newly seduced girl in her brother-in-law's hotel bedroom? Thanks to Fletcher and her own business flair she was a woman to be reckoned with now, not the shy and guilty girl Dorothy had confronted seven years before.

'I knew Kelsey some time ago, yes,' she admitted freely, her hand steady as it closed the gap of her gown over the valley of her breasts. 'It wasn't your business then, just as it isn't now, whether or not Kelsey has one girl or a hundred. I wasn't interested then, and I'm not now, in marrying him. Though it seems to me,' she added contemptuously, turning back to the dresser, 'that your interest in your brother-in-law's affairs is sick, unhealthy. What possible difference can it make to you if Kelsey marries again or not?'

'You don't understand.' Dorothy half ran across the room to lay a fierce grip on Lee's arm. 'It was my duty to split you up that time in San Francisco. Susan was—going through a difficult period then, and Kelsey was—open to other women, other attractions. You're a business woman, can't you understand that it would have been fatal for the Roberts Company if Kelsey had been involved in all the mess of a divorce? He loved Susan, I know he did, but she wasn't easy to live with at that time. Any man presented with temptation when his marriage is going through a difficult period is open to other women, thinking he's made a mistake in marrying the woman who is his wife, but. . . .'

Lee shook the clutching hand from her arm and paced to the safer distance of the bed. Childlike, she wanted to shut out with her hands over her ears what the other woman was saying. She was making excuses for Kelsey, excuses Lee didn't want to hear. It was one thing for herself to dream up reasons for Kelsey's underhandedness, quite another to listen to his virago sister-in-law expounding her views.

'Look,' she said with controlled patience, 'I'm not interested in your brother-in-law's problems, and I don't think you should be either. Why don't you concentrate on your own life, your own marriage, and leave Kelsey to deal with his own affairs? Your husband is an equal partner in the business, isn't he?'

'*Phil!*' Dorothy spat the word contemptuously. 'He doesn't know one end of the boardroom table from the other!' There was an odd sort of protective pride as she faced Lee squarely. 'He should have been an artist, a painter, a writer—anything that doesn't involve corporate decisions! He's useless as a company director, he's not like Kelsey. Sometimes,' she said bitterly, turning jerkily away from Lee's penetrating blue eyes, 'I wonder why Kelsey keeps him on as Marketing Director. Kelsey's a practical man of business, Phil's a dreamer.'

'Maybe Kelsey thinks there's room for dreamers in business, people who think up the ideas for more practical people to put into practice,' Lee said softly, reminded of the visionary haze surrounding several of her own ideas men who had initiated several of the Whitney Company's more successful enterprises. If nothing else on this trip, she was recognising the value of imaginative thinking in her employees; it was a quality she felt she herself lacked, seeing only as far as the factual centre. Maybe, she thought wryly, she and Kelsey had that much in common!

'I'm just afraid,' Dorothy said in an agonised half-whisper, 'that Kelsey will realise, as he hasn't seemed to so far, that Phil is deadweight, that he doesn't contribute to the company as the younger, more with-it college men can. Kelsey can be ruthless, you know,' she added so forlornly that Lee felt a pang of unexpected sympathy for the woman who gave every appearance of being overbearingly managing where her husband was concerned, yet who deeply loved that husband in her own way.

"If he was that ruthless he would have got rid of Phil, brother or not, a long time ago,' Lee pointed out logically. 'Kelsey is first and foremost a business man, and there's no room for dead wood in a business operation. Believe me, he thinks Phil is contributing to the company, or Phil would be out on his ear.'

Dorothy's head lifted from its contemplation of the dressing table surface, and slanted an almost sly look in Lee's direction. 'Is that how you feel too, that Phil's an asset to the company?'

'It's not my business, is it?' Lee shrugged.

'It might be. If—you marry Kelsey. I know him well, and it didn't take me longer than two minutes to know that he's more interested in you than he's been in any woman since Susan——' Dorothy's clawlike fingers played with a small phial of perfume made specially for Lee by a Californian perfumery. 'I think it's possible he still cares for you from those years ago in San Francisco.'

Lee sighed irritably and tossed the hairbrush on to the dresser. The other woman hadn't changed; Lee read her thoughts loud and clear, as if they were emblazoned on her forehead. Dorothy had no real wish to see Kelsey marry again, especially to a woman who could influence him on the merits of keeping his brother on the corporate payroll. But Lee had shown herself to be tolerant in that direction, so now Dorothy was scheming to make an ally of her, Lee.

'Kelsey doesn't even remember that episode in San Francisco,' she said flatly. 'The accident that killed your cousin also disposed of certain of his memories. I haven't told him we met before, and I'd appreciate it if you don't either.'

Dorothy stared her bewilderment. 'He's lost his memory? It's the first I've heard of it.'

'I don't suppose he tells *you* everything,' Lee retorted, gently ironic.

'No, that's true,' the older woman agreed readily and with a tinge of resentment which Lee guessed was of long standing. 'Kelsey's always been very secretive; he didn't even want Susan to confide in me, although God knows the girl needed somebody to confide in at times.'

The hint at Kelsey's marital infidelities was too patent to ignore, but Lee seemed to do just that as she put a hand on the tie belt of her robe.

'If you'll excuse me,' she began pointedly, 'I'm going to be late for dinner if I don't get started now.'

'Oh . . . yes, of course.' Dorothy, already dressed in wine crepe that draped her inadequacies and made the most of her sparse good points, went to the door. Turning back from there, she said in an obsequiously sickening way, 'I'm so glad that we've become friends, that we understand each other. If you and Kelsey ever do get together, it helps to have someone in the family you can talk to.'

Talk to! Lee gritted silently after the door closed on Dorothy's scrawny figure. If Kelsey and his wife had experienced problems in their marriage—and what marriage didn't have problems?—it was for sure they hadn't been helped by Dorothy's interference. If she married Kelsey, the last person she'd confide in would be Dorothy . . .

Lee shook her head in irritation as she took fresh underwear from the drawer. *If* she married Kelsey! There was no possibility of that now or in the future. Susan might have walked into marriage with a man who attracted women like a magnet, but Lee had the foresight to know that any permanent relationship between her and Kelsey wouldn't work. She was too possessive, too needful of the security she could expect from a man like Maitland. . . .

Maitland! She found it hard suddenly to recall his features, his presence. But that didn't matter. Maitland and men like him were the salt of the earth; solid, dependable—dull.

Her hand froze on the hanger holding the white halter-neck dress she intended wearing. Dull!—of course Maitland seemed dull compared with a man like Kelsey. Virtue was always portrayed as being dull; Kelsey's kind was used almost exclusively for ads promoting an exciting, he-man image. Virile, sexy. Dependability came way down on the list for advertising executives.

He wasn't for her, Lee decided again as she walked on slim-heeled shoes across the gallery passage overlooking the living room where every seat surrounding the unlit fireplace seemed to be occupied. Kelsey, in his now familiar stance with his back to the fireplace, seemed to sense her presence as she paused with one hand on the upper rail. Weakness attacked her limbs as their eyes met and the people surrounding him melted into misty oblivion. It was a repeat of that morning, when she had known suddenly and irrevocably that she loved this man as she would no other.

With the same fatalistic certainty, she knew now that she would never marry Maitland.

She blinked and broke the tie binding her eyes to Kelsey's, then moved with dreamlike grace to the stairs. Without a desire to spend her life with Maitland, and the sure knowledge that a permanent relationship with Kelsey could never be, she faced a sterile future with work as her only real satisfaction. She paused on the landing outside Kelsey's study door, her hand lightly touching the thick wood panelling before she dropped it abruptly and straightened her shoulders. There was nothing in her future that she hadn't faced in her past; she had overcome the physical needs Kelsey had sparked briefly into existence, and she could do it again. Her mouth twisted wryly as she started on the downward second flight of red-carpeted stairs. If nothing else, she had that hard-won maturity to thank Kelsey for!

He was waiting at the foot of the stairs, out of view of the assembled company in the living room. His eyes held a warm, appreciative glow as he held out both hands to her in a gesture that would have seemed theatrical in any other man.

'You're beautiful at any time,' he complimented huskily, his eyes dropping to the creamy smoothness of her skin revealed by the narrow band of white halter that rose sleekly from the beginning swell of deep clefted breasts, 'but tonight you're—breathtaking.'

His hands were hard, warm, restrainedly forceful on hers as Lee stared up at him, her resolution of seconds before dissolving momentarily in the thrill that ran from his skin to hers and shivered gooseflesh along her arms. At the same time, a vision flashed in her mind. This was how it might have been, a man greeting with adoring, possessive love the woman he had chosen to spend his life with.

The vision cracked and shattered. Kelsey had looked at another woman in just this way, admiring her beauty before leading her out to play hostess to his family and friends. Susan—the ill-fated beauty who had perhaps loved him in spite of his penchant for young girls. Why else would she have stayed married to him?

A shiver of another kind trembled across her flesh, and she pulled her hands from his, clenching them inaccessibly at her sides.

'Thank you,' she said coolly, stepping sideways past him. 'Is our business talk with Vendisi still on now that your brother and his wife are here?'

She was unprepared for the quick dart of his hand that fastened on the tender flesh of her upper arm and drew her to the hard line of his totally male body.

'Do you practise every day that "touch me not" attitude?' he asked roughly, his breath fanning warmly on her tightly compressed lips. 'Who the hell cares about Vendisi or my brother and his wife?'

Lee's eyes went slowly over his face, every feature intimately open to her view. 'I do,' she said deliberately. 'It's what I came here for, isn't it?'

'No, it damn well isn't,' he gritted with dangerous softness, his hand threatening her neatly coiled hairdo as it fastened on the back of her head. 'I wanted you here for one reason, and one reason only.'

His black eyes streaked hungrily over her face like a man deprived of water for too long in an arid desert. 'I wanted you here for this.' His dark-skinned face swooped suddenly on hers, his fingers digging painfully into her scalp as they levered her head upward to meet the hard crush of his mouth.

He had never kissed her this way before, Lee thought abstractedly as, shocked, she felt the barely restrained violence in him. Her mouth was stiff, unresponsive, when his forceful assault ground her lips against her teeth, hard, hurting. He was punishing her, she recognised dimly, for reasons she could only guess at. Her rigid backbone felt the abrasive touch of his fingers on each nodule as they traced an upward line over the soft material of her dress to the point where fabric ended and firm flesh began.

Amazingly, there was room in her thoughts to wonder what the awaiting company in the living room thought of the protracted delay in their appearance. The low murmur of polite conversation rose and fell against her ears, and then faded into oblivion. The stiff points of Kelsey's fingers left her head and went slowly down to caress her nape, the soft skin on her high-boned cheek, the curving contour of her bared shoulder.

Too real was the heady intoxication his touch evoked. It was softer now, his lips pliant as they pressed in an erotic brush over hers, drawing from them an involuntary response. Her carefully thought out plan to stay cool with Kelsey dissipated like so much mist on a mountain top. Warmth surged, softened, made a clinging focal point of her mouth for the body she pressed helplessly to his, leaning so heedlessly into him that the prominent thrust of her hipbones disappeared into his flesh. Flesh that firmed and hardened even as he pushed her from him, his breath coming in shallow gasps as his heavy-lidded eyes gleamed fiercely into the drugged state of hers.

He cursed with quiet explicitness. 'I've never in my life hated people as much as I do that bunch waiting for us in there.' His hands lifted, settled on the smooth indentation of her waist, dwarfing it. 'But after the meeting. . . .'

The overwhelming desire peaking in Lee made her voice vibrantly husky. 'Yes, I—I'll be in my room.'

The same euphoria followed her into the living room, alarm bells if they were present effectively muzzled by the glow that filled and spilled over from her sparkling eyes, from the graceful lines of her svelte body as she allowed it to be pressed to Kelsey's side, his arm resting lightly on her waist, when they presented themselves to the house guests.

Her eyes first met Dorothy's, which reflected a mixture that struggled between approval and distaste. Was she seeing Susan, the cousin she had mothered, held possessively close by Kelsey? Lee suddenly didn't care. She was going into this relationship with her eyes wide open, prepared for the inevitable rejection at some later date. Wasn't it the 'in' thing to do, to indulge an affair of the senses with no binding ties attached, no promise of permanence?

'I wondered what was keeping you two,' Dorothy said tartly, her brown eyes darting between Kelsey's relaxed possession and Lee's delicately flushed cheeks, 'but I guess I don't have to ask.'

'Ask whatever you like,' Kelsey told her lightly, dropping his arm from around Lee as he asked what she would like to drink.

'Sherry's fine,' she smiled tremulously, and heard his breath draw in on a low note.

'Your wish is my command,' he said in a voice that excluded the others gathered around the fireplace, and she watched bemusedly as his well-knit figure moved smoothly across to the waiting bar. She was being foolish, unrealistic, to let him affect her this way, but long years lay ahead, years when she would turn aside from the high-level dealings of the Whitney Corporation and remember . . . remember this night when Kelsey had loved, desired her.

'I don't feel well,' Bobbi complained when Lee took the seat nearest to the fireplace on the flanking sofa, Harry moodily installed at the far end. 'I knew I shouldn't go on that boat today.'

'You'll be all right,' Lee soothed, although a closer inspection of Bobbi's complexion, discounting the heavy layers of make-up, showed an alarming pastiness. 'You probably still feel a little seasick from the motion of the boat, but——'

'Don't mention the boat,' Bobbi gulped, her free hand clutching at Harry's trouser leg, which he callously brushed off.

'For God's sake, Bobbi,' he said irritably as Kelsey came back to hand Lee her drink, 'you've been on dry land for hours now. There's no way you can feel seasick.'

But Bobbi's skin deepened its pallor as the dinner, highlighted by Lee's salmon catch, progressed. Lee could hardly blame her. The fish caught on her line was even more unacceptable in the eyes of her stomach, dressed up and cooked expertly by the beaming Freda, than it had been lying lifelessly on the deck earlier. Nevertheless, when she was able to obliterate the memory of Kelsey's deft fingers removing the killing hooks from its mouth, she admitted grudgingly to herself that it did taste good. The orange-pink flesh broke moistly to her fork, and it was obvious that the Roberts family, including Dorothy, enjoyed the fruit of the sea with serene contentment.

'I've never been interested in fishing myself,' Dorothy confided to the table at large, 'but I've always thought it must be a great satisfaction to a man,' she stressed, 'to bring home an acceptable meal for his family.'

'Is the sex of the food provider important?' Kelsey asked the table at large in his bland, non-assertive voice. 'Personally, I don't give a damn whether the fish was caught by a man or a woman or a child, it's just plain good.'

While the others bent their heads over their plates in imitation of his, Lee looked round the table and caught Harry Vendisi's eye. There was speculation there, and a palpable assessment as the mud brown eyes went heavily between her and the blissfully unconcerned Kelsey, who was making quite a production of his enjoyment of the fish. Her gaze swivelled back to rest on Kelsey's black head bent over his plate. Was it possible that his mild façade covered a deep down business sense that told him not only Frantug, but Vendisi's lucrative shipping business could be his if he handled her, Lee, in the right way? That way, despite his seemingly non-chauvinistic façade, which would gain for him all the advantages of a man in control . . . a play on the female emotions Lee had made only too clear she was prey to.

She felt alone suddenly, alone in a bewildering sea of deal and counter-deal, where ethics were pushed aside in favour of financial gain. Their name was legion in the world she moved in, but Kelsey wasn't like them . . . was he?

His eyes lifted then and looked with disconcerting straightness into hers. It was as if he sensed, knew, the doubts assailing her, the desperate need she felt to believe in something, someone.

The moment went as quickly as it had come, drowned in the surge of conversation between one course and the other. Lee made a purposeful effort to push aside the doubts assailing her and was surprised at how easily the facile flow of socially orientated words tripped smoothly from her lips.

'Yes,' she said in answer to Dorothy's politely worded question, 'I was brought up near San Francisco. My father built up a charter airline that covered most of California. He had been a pilot in the second world war, and he never lost that yen to take off into the wide blue yonder.'

'Thank God I wasn't old enough to take part in a useless war that proved nothing,' Harry interposed brusquely. '*My* father was killed in that war, and for what?'

Lee's gaze swung back to his belligerently set jaw, seeing a little of the powers that motivated him.

'Maybe he wanted to give you the right to choose your life-style, rather than having one imposed on you,' she reminded him with a touch of irony.

'I really feel sick,' Bobbi pronounced out of the blue, her portion of Lee's catch untouched on the plate before her. She pushed back her chair suddenly, and looked appealingly at Harry. 'I really feel sick, Harry. I'm going up to my room.'

Harry did no more than glare at her as she stumbled from her place and went with lowered head towards the stairs.

'Maybe I should see if there's something I can do,' Dorothy, in her role of chatelaine, rose to say.

'There's no need,' Harry quelled her so that she sat down again abruptly. 'She wants attention, that's all, and I'll be damned if I supply on demand.'

Anger surged in a hot wave through Lee, but even as her lips opened to speak Kelsey intervened quietly.

'Bobbi hasn't been feeling well since this morning, Harry, when we went out on the boat. Maybe you should check on her.'

'I tell you there's nothing wrong with her,' Harry reiterated belligerently, his dark brows beetling in Kelsey's direction. 'You hit the nail on the head when you mentioned the boat—she didn't want to go this morning, and she wouldn't have if I hadn't made her. She's just trying to prove something, and it has nothing to do with anybody here.' His baleful brown eyes flickered round the table and settled on Lee who, uncowed, pushed back her chair with an unhurried gesture.

'I have to go upstairs anyway,' she offered coolly. 'I'll need my notebook for our discussions later on, and I can check on Bobbi while I'm up there.'

She was aware of four pairs of eyes appraising her in varying degrees as she left the room and went determinedly towards the stairs. Cold fury accompanied her when she thought of the unfortunate Bobbi, caught in a situation with a man who cared no more for her than he would for some minor personality in his business organisation.

Why would a woman have so little self-respect as to allow a man, any man, to treat her this way? Bobbi's relationship with Harry Vendisi smacked of a bygone age, when a woman had no recourse but to have a man take care of and protect her. The strong spirit of independence in Lee brought her mouth down in a disapproving curve as she stepped quickly across the upper hall to the bedroom area lying in the opposite direction to her own. The rooms in this corridor were unfamiliar to her, but a tentative second knock brought Bobbi's subdued, 'Come in.'

The blonde girl was lying on one of the large twin beds stationed between two windows, her rounded cheeks matching the colour of the tufted spread.

'I wondered if there's anything I can get for you,' Lee asked gently, hiding the genuine flash of concern in her eyes. The girl really did seem to be ill; although Bobbi's acceptance of her life with Harry Vendisi was hard for Lee to understand, sympathy had struck an unexpected chord of protectiveness.

'No, thanks, I'll be okay,' Bobbi refused faintly, turning her head aside on the pillows. 'I've—felt this way before, and it goes away. I'll be okay by morning.'

Lee stared down at her averted face worriedly. 'I

don't know what Kelsey does about getting a doctor
out here, but——'

'No doctor!' Bobbi's head whipped back, her
voice suddenly strong. 'Harry hates sickness and all
the fuss.'

'Too bad for Harry,' Lee said silently to herself.
Aloud, she asked quietly, 'Why do you do it, Bobbi?'

The round blue eyes looked up at her in question.
'Do what?'

'Live with Harry the way you do, let him treat you
the way he does. Look, I know it's not my business,
but——'

'No, that's true,' Bobbi agreed, but she seemed not
to have enough strength to feel angry about it. 'I
guess you're wondering why we don't get married
and make it all nice and legal.'

That hadn't been the point of her question at all,
but Lee kept silent. It wasn't her business, and she
had no right to pry.

'Harry wants to marry me, but he can't get a
divorce,' Bobbi said wearily, missing Lee's sceptically
lifted brows. 'It's against his religion. I know it
sounds funny for a man like Harry to feel that way,
but he does. He was brought up that way and it stuck.
I don't think about marriage any more now. Why
should I? I have everything else I want.'

Smoothing the skirt of her dress behind her, Lee sat
down on the edge of the bed and looked at the fair
girl with perplexed concern. 'You can't mean that
you're content to live this way? What about the time
when Harry decides he wants a change, what happens to you then?'

Bobbi's eyes widened in genuine astonishment. 'Why should he want a change? He loves me—and believe it or not, he needs me even more than I need him.'

Love! Lee bit her lip in irritation. How could a person reason with someone as gullible and naïve as Bobbi? Scorn tinged her. 'And I suppose you love him too.'

'Of course.' Bobbi summoned up a smile, and had the gall to shake her head commiseratingly. 'You're not much younger than me, are you, Lee, but you don't know too much about people, do you? Oh, I know you run a fancy business down there in San Francisco, and I couldn't do that, but I'm pretty good at reading people. For instance, that Kelsey—he's crazy about you, but you give him the cold treatment all the time.' Some colour had come back into her cheeks, and one of them dimpled when her smile deepened. 'You're passing up a man every tycoon's daughter in Seattle has her heart set on. But I never heard of him getting serious about anybody—once bitten, twice shy, I guess.'

Lee started. 'Wh—what do you mean by that?'

'Didn't you know he'd been married?'

'Yes.'

'Well, that was one marriage that wasn't made in heaven!' Bobbi seemed to have recovered most of her animation as she went on, 'She was no good for a man like Kelsey—or any other man, from what I hear. She was very beautiful, and very ladylike with it, but she was still a——'

'I'm not too interested in Kelsey's wife,' Lee said

dishonestly, rising hastily. She *was* interested in Susan Roberts, devastatingly, gnawingly interested in the woman Kelsey had been married to even as he made love to her seven years ago. She didn't want to hear bad things about her, because that would make Kelsey's actions partly excusable. Admitting to herself that she loved him was one thing; forgiving him was something she could never do.

Half-turned away when Bobbi spoke again, she swung back to stare into the knowing yet innocent blue eyes.

'I don't believe that,' Bobbi said softly. 'You see, I've been watching you too, and I know you're as crazy about him as he is about you.'

CHAPTER SEVEN

'THAT's the deal, take it or leave it.' Harry leaned back in the black leather tub chair in front of Kelsey's neat-topped desk. Addressing Kelsey, as he had during most of their negotiations, he went on, 'I don't have to tell you that when the word gets out that Venmar is open to the highest bidder, a lot of people will jump at the chance.'

The comfortable study, adequate but without extraneous frills, faded from Lee's consciousness as she battled internally with Harry Vendisi's ridiculously high figure in addition to the grating note of his chauvinistic belief that held a woman unable to speak on behalf of a corporation as powerful as Whitney's. Kelsey, his eyes hooded as he leaned back in his chair behind the desk, had been his usual quiet, attentive self as Harry expounded the virtues of owning and operating a lucrative export–import business in that part of the United States.

'You're way out of line, Harry,' Kelsey said just as quietly as he had conducted himself throughout the evening, but now as Lee's eyes lifted to his she saw the cold, steely gleam glinting off them and realised abstractedly that the Roberts Company hadn't risen to its present status with a pussyfooting President at its helm. 'Venmar might be worth close to half of what you're asking, but of course I have to consult with my partner on what we think it's worth to us in real terms.'

'Well, sure,' Harry blustered, running a thick finger between his collar and neck, 'I can't think why you didn't ask your brother in here in the first place.'

'I wasn't referring to my brother,' Kelsey returned quietly, his eyes flickering across to Lee. 'Lee represents the Whitney Corporation, and they would be putting up the bigger part of the money for this kind of operation.'

'Now look, I've no objection to having a woman sit in on our talks, but you can't expect her to make a decision as important as this.' Harry looked at Lee as if she were a child unable to understand adult conversation. 'Women aren't made that way.'

'No,' Lee agreed sweetly, 'our intelligence is limited to the diaper pail and the dust that accumulates on the furniture our men labour to provide for us.' Her voice hardened. 'If that's so, then the Whitney Corporation would still be content with a San Francisco Bay tug company and a few minor investments! It was a woman who lifted Whitney's out of mediocrity, Mr Vendisi—me! And it's on my say-so if you happen to sell your operation here tonight.'

Her eyes flew immediately to Kelsey, gauging his reaction to her headily spoken words. He had much more at stake than she did in acquiring Venmar. It would be a glittering jewel in the Roberts Company crown, just another lucrative addition to the Whitney Corporation. To her oddly inflated relief, she saw a smile twitch at the corners of Kelsey's mouth.

'So there you have it, Harry,' he said equably,

rising lithely to his feet to indicate that the meeting was over. 'Lee and I will talk about it and come up with a counter-offer in the morning.'

'You know something?' Harry lumbered to his feet and looked Kelsey squarely in the eye. 'I admire a man who can let a woman dictate to him, in business or anything else. Because it means he doesn't give a damn what real men think of him!'

Stomping from the room before Kelsey had time to make a reply, Harry made his exit trailing a cloud of blue cigar smoke behind him. The room was quiet suddenly without his presence, and Lee felt strangely constrained as she looked across the desk into Kelsey's harshly contoured features.

'It isn't true, you know,' she offered into the silence. 'Men these days don't have to beat their chests and twang their arrows to assert themselves as men.'

He said nothing as he rounded the desk and came to pull her up from the chair that matched Harry's on the other side of the desk. 'I know,' he said simply, huskily, his hands searing their warmth through the flimsy white of her dress, drawing her to the angled maleness of his body. 'But you can't tell Harry that.' His head bent to gain access to the white column of her throat, and the touch of his warm lips on her flesh started a chain of shivering reaction that trembled as far as her toes in the sleekly elegant frontless pumps and vibrated upward again to the brain that told her she was being foolishly susceptible to the charms that had ensnared so many women over the years—too many women. But no effort of will could stem the golden glow of frank desire that followed the path of his lips to the taut cord at her neck, to the sensually arousing press of his mouth at the dimpled crease at hers, the inexorable building of a tension Lee found herself unable to handle. Yet . . . her mouth shaped itself to the urgent pressure of his as if it had a life of its own, her hands moulding the white shirt stretched across his warm muscled chest, feeling the virile strength of him, trying vainly to deny it.

'Kelsey, please, I——'

'I know.' He left her mouth to kiss lightly the tip of her small straight nose, the curve of her cheekbones, the hollows beside her eyes. 'This isn't the time, or the place, but soon it will be. You're driving me crazy,' he said huskily at her ear, then drew back to look quizzically down into her eyes. 'You look so cool, so—indifferent. But underneath you're like a dia-mond—hidden fires, hidden depths.'

Lee pulled away, finally and reluctantly, her flesh still hot from his touch as she went without words from the room and stepped on light feet the short flight of stairs leading to the upper floor.

She loved him, she exulted, and not even the solid disapproval of the ancient armoires lining the upper passage dimmed the tingling excitement shivering through her veins. The past was a dead element in her mind, the future a hazy mélange of possibilities. Nothing mattered at this moment more than that Kelsey would come to her, make love to her, possess the parts of her that had lain dormant for so long . . . too long.

The hard stinging spray of the shower forced her

mind into other channels of thought. Kelsey's lack of enthusiasm for Harry Vendisi's deal could indicate that his company was far from being dependent on any added acquisitions. On the other hand, Kelsey might feel he had more lucrative fish to fry in another direction. From their first meeting on the terrace for the English tea which Freda had amply provided, he had made it known that marriage was in his future. Not some far-off, hazy event, but a pending arrangement he took for granted.

Thoughtfully, Lee shut off the taps and stepped from the tub, reaching for the thick towel she employed with pensive strokes to dry herself.

Would a man soon to marry someone behave as Kelsey had towards her? There had been no mention since of the woman he expected to make his wife. Instead, there had been a—calculated?—assault on her, Lee's, senses. Was it possible Kelsey had been talking about her as the woman he meant to marry? The thought stilled her hands in mid-motion as they chafed the towel across her white skin.

Kelsey remembered nothing of their previous encounters in San Francisco all those years ago. Why, then, would he want to marry her?

The answer to that was only too simple, Lee thought savagely as she tugged the waist belt of her robe around her and stepped stiffly into the bedroom, pulling the pins from her hair with quick motions as she regarded her stiffly set features in the dressing table mirror. Kelsey had set out on a deliberate campaign to woo, not Lee Whitney but Whitney Enterprises in their entirety! The Frantug operation,

which he had been so anxious to procure years ago,
had become a mere stepping stone to greater things.
As the husband of Lee Whitney, an entire new world
would open up to him, a world encompassing all Lee
had accomplished since Fletcher's death.

There was nothing new to Lee in the realisation
that a man who showed amorous interest in her was
governed by the prospect of great wealth accumulat-
ing to him from any liaison. Anger, spawned from
hurt, leapt through Lee's veins.

It was her own fault, she reminded herself as she
applied a vicious brush to her cascading hair.
Prompted by the remembered love of long ago, she
had been only too willing to respond to Kelsey's
renewed advances. He, on the other hand, had no
memory of that time, no heartwrenching sorrow at
the loss of his child, no regrets that while he was
married he turned the life of a young girl upside
down and left her with bitterness and hatred in her
heart.

'You look beautiful.'

Lee started violently and dropped the brush on the
dresser top with a hollow ring as she turned to see
Kelsey, as fresh from the shower as she herself was,
standing with his back to the door in short red silk
robe. Speechless, she followed the progress of his
lean muscled male legs across the scarlet carpet.
Rising, up beyond the crisply virile vee of black hair
on his chest, her eyes met the dark sheen of his. He
was a being fashioned from a woman's fantasies, tall,
strong, with all the latent strength of sensuality in his
primitively set cheekbones, the jut of his smoothly
shaved jaw.

'Kelsey, I——'

'Don't talk.' His finger laid an admonishing stroke on the soft, smooth outline of her lips. 'I know you've been thinking about it—you, me, us—and I want you to know that this isn't just one of those things that happen in passing. I love you, Lee, and I want to marry you.' His hands, warm and smooth, slid down over her silk robe and clasped at her waist. 'I've waited a long time for somebody like you, Lee. You're everything I ever dreamed of in a woman.'

A bubble of hysterical laughter was stifled immediately in Lee's throat, and there was nothing of humour in her eyes when they met Kelsey's. He seemed sincere; but then wouldn't he seem just as sincere if his motive wasn't a deep and abiding love for her but an even deeper commitment to strengthen his own company by aligning it with Whitney's?

'Well?' he asked, half teasing, his fingers sliding under her chin to lift her fallen view to his again. 'Do you usually take this long to consider marriage proposals?'

Lee saw her opening and took it. 'No, because usually I'm very sure of the man's motives in asking me to marry him. Mostly it's because he's dazzled by the Whitney brilliance, not my personal charms.' Sarcasm edged her dry tone, and she saw Kelsey's eyes narrow, his body tense against hers.

'And what decision have you come to about my motives?' he asked, dangerously quiet.

Shrugging, Lee moved out of his slackened arms, tightening the belt of her robe as she put space between them. Kelsey stood rock still, watching her intently.

'I'm not sure,' she answered honestly. 'We haven't known each other that long, have we?'

'Long enough for you to be willing to come to bed with me,' he pointed out with harsh logic. 'Or is sex a part of your life you keep strictly separated from your precious Whitney's? Did the old man you married state in his will that you'd lose it if you married again?'

Lee whirled on him furiously. 'Fletcher wouldn't do such a thing! He—he *wanted* me to marry again.'

'But he also warned you to beware of wolves in sheep's clothing? Like me?'

'Fletcher was like a——'

'A father to you?' Kelsey cut in with a grim kind of satisfaction. 'Or were you about to say grandfather?'

Lee's breath drew in sharply on a pain she had thought was behind her now. She had weathered the storms of frigid disapproval from San Francisco society at the time of her marriage to Fletcher; he had warned her to expect it, but her pain had been on his behalf, not her own.

'I think you'd better go,' she said, turning her back to the impassively scornful Kelsey.

'You're right there,' he returned nastily, turning back from the door to add, his voice cold, 'And I'd like to thank you.'

'Thank me?' Lee looked round in surprise, her hair falling in a shimmering curtain beside her cheek. 'For what?'

'For turning me down. I'm sweating at the thought that you might have accepted me, and I'd be tied to a corporate machine plugged into a computer terminal! I don't make many mistakes, Lee, but it seems I made a colossal blunder with you. As I said——'

His voice tapered off as a thunderous knocking sounded from somewhere outside. 'Kelsey! Kelsey!' Harry's voice came clearly through Lee's door. 'For God's sake, wake up and help me.'

Lee held up an automatically cautioning hand, but Kelsey threw wide her door, disregarding the compromising picture he presented in the short robe that made clear his nudity under it. But Harry, she realised a second later, was in no state to remark on his host's propriety or lack of it.

'Kelsey, it's Bobbi, she's really sick. We have to get a doctor over here.'

'Okay, okay,' Kelsey soothed, taking the other man's arm in a hard grasp. 'But it might be better if we can get her to a hospital. Can she be moved?'

'Moved? For God's sake, man, she's in agony!' Harry cried.

'If it's what I think it is, there's no point in bringing a doctor over to the island. She'll need an operation, and he can't do that here.'

Harry's florid complexion paled. 'Operation? Oh, my God!'

'You go back to her,' Kelsey ordered firmly, 'while I get dressed and get the boat ready.' He turned back to Lee, who had come to stand behind him, and said tersely as Harry half-ran along the passage, 'You'd better get dressed too. Harry won't be of much use to her in the state he's in.'

Lee nodded. 'What is it you think is wrong with her?'

'Appendix,' he returned briefly, already across the hall and throwing open the door to his own room. 'Hurry, Lee, we've got to get her over there as soon as possible. I'll alert the hospital on my way out to the boat.'

There was no time for panic or trembling. Lee was, anyway, at her best in a crisis, only feeling its effects when the crucial time had passed. She dressed swiftly in warm slacks and sweater top, catching up a suede jacket as she passed the closet on her way out.

Bobbi was sitting up on the bed hugging her knees, her round face deathly white, even more so than it had been earlier that evening, but her eyes flashed relief when Lee came up beside the bed.

'Kelsey's getting the boat ready,' Lee said soothingly, 'and he's alerted the hospital at the other side, so in a little while you'll be okay. Is there anything I can do for you right now?'

Bobbi's lips twisted in an agonised smile as she nodded to Harry, who was pacing worriedly back and forth at the far side of the room. 'Just take care of Harry,' she whispered jerkily. 'He's worse than a father with his first baby.'

Lee was in the midst of marvelling that Bobbi, even in dire pain, thought only of Harry's welfare when Kelsey strode into the room, his legs encased in jeans, his plaid casual shirt barely visible under the cotton windbreaker he wore. Reaching the bed, he bent over and gave Bobbi a reassuring grin.

'Aren't I the lucky one? I get to carry the princess

to her carriage. Now I'm going to wrap this blanket around you, and I want you to put your arms around my neck. That's it. Okay, honey?'

Bobbi nodded, her lower lip caught between her teeth. Kelsey lost no time, striding out as rapidly as he had entered the room, as if Bobbi's weight was nothing. Harry, still dressed formally, trotted along behind, Lee bringing up the rear.

Ever after, that journey seemed a nightmare to Lee. Ensconced on one of the two bunks the cruiser boasted, Bobbi writhed deliriously in pain while Lee berated her own failure to follow her earlier instinct and make Kelsey call a doctor. This crisis might have been averted that way, although by the time a doctor arrived on the island and ordered her removal, little time would have been saved. But Kelsey had obviously suspected appendicitis earlier—why hadn't he made the arrangements then? Lee knew little or nothing of medical complications, but she was aware that an inflamed appendix could develop into something a lot more serious.

The twenty-minute journey seemed to take three times that long that night as she sponged Bobbi's feverish forehead with cool water drawn from the tiny galley sink. Relief surged through her when at last Kelsey, who had thoughtfully kept the distraught Harry up top beside him, came down to tell them they had arrived.

'There's an ambulance waiting,' he told Lee as he scooped up the half unconscious Bobbi from the bunk and hurried up the short flight of steps to the deck. Lee, following closely, saw the white-jacketed attendants waiting at the dockside with a stretcher, and a great weight seemed to lift from her as they lowered Bobbi to it and strapped her on before hurrying towards the white ambulance at the end of the dock.

She swayed lightheadedly, and felt a strong arm go round her, a familiar smooth-muscled chest beneath her cheek for an instant.

'Will she be all right?' she asked faintly, as if Kelsey were the oracle who knew all things.

'I hope so,' his voice rumbled grimly under her ear. 'I blame myself that I didn't get her over here earlier, but some people have a grumbling appendicitis for years without it getting to the acute stage.'

'If anyone should have known, it was Harry,' Lee consoled, lifting her head reluctantly though she was glad that Kelsey's arm remained firmly, reassuringly, round her. 'Bobbi told me when I went to see her earlier that she's had these bouts before, but Harry hates her to be sick, so she downplayed them.'

Kelsey echoed Bobbi's words of a few hours before. 'Well, of course he hates her to be sick. He loves her, he's terrified of losing her.'

'Have you ever loved anyone so much that you were terrified of losing her?' Lee asked without conscious thought and immediately wished she could draw the words back. Of course he had loved his wife, Susan, and he had known her loss. It must be worse for him because he had been driving the car in the accident that took her life.

'Yes,' he responded briefly, dropping his arm from her so that she was forced to stand upright on her own, 'and I did lose her.' His eyes reflected the glint of moonlight as they slanted down to her upraised face. 'There's more than one way of losing a person you care about. But you wouldn't know about that, would you, Mrs Whitney?'

The last words stung, and Lee blinked defensively. What were they talking about? Loss of a loved one through illness, death—or her doubts about his motives for asking her to marry him?

He seemed to expect no answer, however, going on in the hard, precise tone she was beginning to recognise, 'Shall we go home, or join Harry's vigil at the hospital? My own feeling is that it won't do him one bit of harm to sweat it out on his own for a while. He takes Bobbi all too much for granted, in my opinion.'

Lee looked curiously up at him, unaware that the fitful moon made mysterious magic of her eyes, and glinted white-gold bands around her hair, which still fell untrammelled at either side of her face.

'Home,' she opted, and felt a sense of letdown when Kelsey went determinedly to the wheel amidships and fired the motor to purring quietness.

She sat on the gunwale seats behind him as he steered the lively craft towards the island, her eyes never leaving the tall lean strength of him, the well-shaped head with its thick black hair touched to silver where the moon glanced off it. How much longer would she be within sight, within touch of him? Her eyes fell to the rhythmic swell pushed back by the boat's powerful thrust through the water. What had she done that night, before Harry had alerted them to Bobbi's illness?

Her thoughts flowed as clear as the moonlight that

sent its complacent glow down to the earth underneath it. She loved Kelsey, would always love him
whatever her future brought. Did it really matter
that his interest might be more in Whitney's than in
her? Her trouble was, she thought forlornly, that her
personality seemed to have split way back, seven
years ago when she had woven all those dreams
around Kelsey and the life they would have together.
The deepest, most innocent part of her still wanted
that; marriage, a home she would make beautiful for
both of them, children ... her eyes lifted involuntarily to the broad outline of Kelsey's back, the
rippling movement of his muscles as he veered the
boat round towards the island. Their child would
have been six years old; would he have been pleased
about the news that he was to be a father? He had
never had other children with his wife. Maybe he
didn't care for them, didn't need them to round out
his life with Susan.

Susan ... the beautiful, fun-loving wife he had
adored. The wife he had thought to replace with the
President of Whitney Enterprises! The other part of
her split personality was just that. Cool, efficient Mrs
Whitney, her finger on the pulse of every operation
in Whitney's far-flung empire. A poised woman,
antennae alert for signs of self-seeking on the part of
those she did business with.

Self-seeking. Was Kelsey that? Proposing marriage
to a woman he knew could bring him power most
men only dreamed of must surely be self-seeking?
Yet ... he had shown restraint, almost disinterest, in
Harry's business deal, a deal which might have

brought the Roberts Company into even more prominence in the shipping world.

Starkly, Lee recalled Kelsey's face when she had voiced her doubts. The lines marking his eyes and mouth had deepened, ageing him and giving him a stricken look in contrast to the more usual confident set of his features. It was the look, more than any other, that would follow her down all the years to come. As if she, Lee, had struck him a mortal body blow.

'Were you intending to spend the night here?' Kelsey's voice interrupted her train of thought and she started, looking round disbelievingly at the darkly outlined dock beside them, the erratic pinpoints of light coming from the half-sleeping household up the slope.

'No,' she retorted sharply, venting the annoyance she felt with her own muddled thinking on him. Rising, she accepted the rough warmth of his hand as he helped her from boat to dock.

She waited while Kelsey secured the gently undulating vessel, turning to walk towards the house when he joined her on the wood planking of the pier.

Silence accompanied their trek up to the house along the bark-strewn trail, and it was only when Kelsey slid aside the patio doors into the living room that he spoke.

'I'll make us some coffee, I'm sure you feel the need of it as much as I do.'

Not knowing what else to do, Lee followed him to the kitchen at the rear of the house and looked round interestedly at the efficiently laid out work centres

positioned for the cook's greatest convenience. As
Kelsey reached for the coffee pot hanging from a
series of pegs positioned over a counter between sink
and stove, she sauntered across to the central cloth-
covered table and sat down on one of the four straight
backed chairs flanking it.

There was something cosily reassuring in the
sounds Kelsey made as he went from stove to refrigerator and back to the cupboard over the sink
from which he extracted man-sized mugs and joined
them to saucers laid ready. Her life had been far
removed from kitchens and domesticity these past
years; thinking of Hannah's reaction if Lee had ventured into the lofty kitchen of the San Francisco
house brought an unconscious smile to her mouth as
she absently watched Kelsey's straight-backed movements.

What was there about him that made her think of
kitchens and cooking and—yes, a pot of flowers on a
red-checked gingham cloth? Even now, so far
removed from girlish dreams, it wasn't hard to imagine her eyes watching him as he ate, alert for the
slightest betraying sign of pleasure or its reverse as he
sampled the offerings she had cooked with her own
hand. Sighing, she reflected with dry inner humour
that none of the men or the few women she did
business with would believe that, under her coolly
competent façade, there still lurked a starry-eyed
romantic girl!

Yet love didn't have to encompass the basic ritual
give-and-take of marriage. Bobbi and Harry, for instance . . . hardly recovered from Bobbi's obviously

sincere declaration of love for Harry, her mind had reeled again at his genuine display of concern for Bobbi. No man who cared that much for a woman, albeit she was his mistress with no legal attachment, could be accused of not loving her. It wasn't the kind of life Lee had ever contemplated for herself; perhaps because of her background with parents who lived for each other and their child, she knew that she could never be satisfied with anything less than that kind of undying commitment. Sadly, she wondered if Bobbi had felt that way once, too.

'Is it permissible for a junior partner to enquire about the source of all these sighs and pensive looks?' Kelsey interrupted her thoughts, and Lee started, focusing vaguely on the red, black and white check of his shirt, opened at the neck to reveal the wiry black swirl of chest hairs that reached up towards the well-shaped column of his neck.

'I was just thinking,' she said spontaneously, 'how much Harry and Bobbi love each other.'

His brows lifted in a dark arc over eyes that displayed tiny pinpoints of yellow light. 'You sound surprised. Do you think they'd have stayed together as long as they have without being in love with each other?'

Confused, Lee dropped her eyes from the penetratingly uncomfortable regard in his. 'I thought Bobbi was being foolishly dependent,' she admitted frankly, 'on a man who could provide her with all the goodies in the candy store without offering her the thing that means most to a woman.'

'Such as?'

Lee lifted her eyes, blinked, and said, 'Security,' she shrugged, 'a sense of belonging, building a life together, having children and—bringing them up together.'

'A lot of people are not interested in bringing up children, they're content with each other.'

As you were with Susan? Lee cried inwardly. Suddenly she was fiercely, acidly glad that her child hadn't lived to know that its father was indifferent to its existence. Glad that Kelsey had never become the husband of her stupidly romantic girlish dreams. If she had known him better seven years ago, how different her life might have been now! She might have been married to a man who would love her and the children they created from that love. The fulfilment Whitney Enterprises had given her in the intervening years faded into insignificance beside the personal satisfaction of loving and being loved, giving and receiving the intimate commitment there could be between two people.

The impetus of her thoughts sent her upright, the chair scraping on the waxed tiles. But she had taken only a few steps towards the kitchen door when Kelsey caught up with her, swinging her round to face him so that her hands went in an instinctively steadying motion to the pulsing warmth of his chest, her carefully manicured fingers bracing her against the vivid checks of his shirt.

'What's the matter, Lee?' he asked, his voice a hard jeer. 'Does it bother Madame President to think about the kind of love Harry and Bobbi have? Or was it the mention of children that made you realise how

empty your life really is? But it could be I'm cynical—maybe you and your faithful right-hand man
are planning at least one son to take over your combined interests when the time comes.'

Lee stared speechlessly, her tongue frozen but her
thoughts roaming freely. How often had Maitland
projected into the future and seen his own son stepping, after a suitable education, into his own shoes? A
son who would not only bear the noble name of Fra-
zier, but who would fall heir to the burgeoning
wealth of Whitney's.

'Most men want a son to carry on their name,'
she defended, wanting more than ever to be gone
from this room, from Kelsey's overwhelming presence. She would leave tomorrow, she thought
wildly; how much easier it was to hate him from a
distance!

'Most men want a child from the woman they
love,' he pointed out levelly, his hands warm and firm
now on the spare flesh of her ribcage, 'not for the sole
reason of keeping the wealth in the family.'

'What would you know about it?' Lee cried wildly,
her back taut against his confining hands. 'You didn't
see fit to have children with your wife, although you
were married for—years.' Her voice faded at the last
word, and her eyes dropped from the narrowed fires
in his.

'No.'

There was just the one word, and the hard inflection he used might have meant anything. Regret that
he had no visible symbol of the marriage of years,
or—but that was too ridiculous. He had loved Susan

so much that he must have wanted their child. But perhaps——

'Couldn't your wife have children?' she murmured, conscience-stricken now that she might have touched a raw spot in Kelsey's psyche which had not yet healed.

'Susan was as capable as any other woman,' Kelsey returned without emotion. 'She just didn't care to, as she termed it, spoil her figure.' His hand covered, almost abstractedly, the smooth line of Lee's abdomen. 'And maintaining her figure was of prime importance to Susan.'

Lee's spine stiffened against the hand that remained there, resenting the power it held over her senses but unable to take the vital step that would remove her from his orbit. She didn't want to hear derogatory statements about Susan; they brought the dead woman too close, too real, for comfort. Yet some basic woman instinct craved the assurance that Kelsey's wife had not been the epitome of satisfaction Lee had imagined her to be.

The percolator's sudden silence indicated that the coffee was ready, and Kelsey dropped his arms from her and went to fill the waiting mugs with its aromatic brew. Lee groped for and found the smooth wooden back of the chair she had abandoned minutes earlier and sank into it, her legs trembling with unaccustomed nervousness. The kitchen seemed all at once to have an oppressive air, an atmosphere of thoughts unspoken which imbued it with a mystery she found unsettling.

'Susan didn't care for children,' or people and

situations she considered boring,' Kelsey resumed as if there had been no break in the conversation, his hands deft as they placed coffee before Lee and offered her cream and sugar. 'Spending time with me here on the island was the most classic bore of all for her.'

'I—I really don't want to hear this,' Lee protested faintly. 'It doesn't concern me.'

'Doesn't it?' Kelsey asked tersely, his hand falling on hers across the table and twisting it into her grasp. 'You're wrong, Lee, it has everything to do with you—me—us. I've asked you to marry me, and that gives you the right to know certain things about my first marriage.'

'No, it doesn't,' Lee said desperately. 'I turned you down, remember?'

There was a pause of silence, then Kelsey said, low and hurriedly: 'That was because I haven't been completely honest with you. You see, Lee, there are reasons why I——'

His voice was cut off in mid-sentence by the sudden opening of the door and Dorothy's appearance in its frame. The pale pink of her terry wrapper did nothing to enhance her blotchy complexion and her brown eyes seemed more muddy than ever as they went between Kelsey and Lee and down to the entwined clasp of their hands.

'I thought I heard voices down here. What in the world is going on, Kelsey? There's been so much noise going on in this house tonight that I've hardly been able to get a wink of sleep.'

Briefly, Kelsey explained the midnight mercy

errand with Bobbi, his hand still firmly gripped on Lee's, who tried in vain to release it.

'Oh . . . I see,' said Dorothy when Kelsey stopped speaking. 'Well, I knew there was something wrong with the girl at dinner tonight. I wanted to do something about it then, but everyone else seemed to think I was interfering unnecessarily.' She heaved a martyr's sigh and was turning back to the hall when her eyes fell again on the closeness of Kelsey's grip on Lee's hand. 'Well, as they say,' she smirked, 'it's an ill wind that blows nobody any good. At least you two have been brought together by the emergency. And not before time, I might add. I was finding it very difficult to remember that you had supposedly had a blackout about knowing Lee all that time ago in San Francisco, Kelsey. I knew all the time, of course, that your memory wasn't impaired at all in the accident. But,' she shrugged and smiled with smug piety, 'I don't interfere in matters that don't concern me.'

'I hadn't noticed that that was one of your virtues,' Kelsey said with a quiet irony that was lost on Dorothy as she pulled the door closed behind her. Apart from the perceptible tightening of his fingers on Lee's, he had received Dorothy's statement without question.

CHAPTER EIGHT

THERE was silence in the kitchen apart from the refrigerator's cycle which started up and hummed rhythmically. Lee's eyes were transfixed on the slender whiteness of her fingers overlaid with the stark contrast of Kelsey's brown skin.

He knew, she reflected dully, remembered that time seven years ago when he had been the sun of her existence. Yet he had said nothing, given no indication that he recalled that shriven bond between them. Why? Why?

Her eyes lifted, reflecting in their clear, intense blue the gigantic question filling her mind. Impersonally they noted the belligerent tilt of his darkly shadowed chin, the taut compression of his mouth, the eyes that burned with liquid fire when her own rose to meet them.

'Why?' she echoed her thought faintly. 'Why, Kelsey?'

'Would you have come up here to my island if you'd known who I was?' he asked hoarsely.

'I knew who you were,' she returned, bewilderment clouding her eyes. 'I came to—to——'

'You came to pay me back for what I did to you in San Francisco all those years ago, didn't you?'

'Yes,' she admitted helplessly, 'yes, I did.'

His eyes contracted in obvious pain. 'Don't you

think I knew that?' he asked, anguished. 'The only way I could think of to keep you here was to pretend I'd lost some parts of my memory, that I didn't remember you at all. I wanted to give myself time to woo you all over again. I even arranged that Freda should believe the accident left me with blind spots in my memory.' His mouth turned down wryly. 'I didn't realise, of course, that Dorothy would show up while you were here on the island.'

Feeling started to come back to her brain, her sinews, her veins; with it came her mind's remembrance of all the hurts, abrasions, Kelsey had carved like a brand on her senses.

'Why me?' she choked. 'There were other girls in your life while you were married to Susan. Why single me out now?'

She saw the dull gleam of comprehension far back in her eyes. 'You think I've selected you from the crowd because you're who you are?' His hands crushed hers with emotional force. 'There were no other girls, Lee,' he said softly. 'I know it was wrong to make love to you, you were so young and sweet and loving, and I was married at the time. Not happily, but that doesn't excuse what I let happen between us.' He released her fingers suddenly, leaving them white and bloodless as he pushed back his chair and moved restlessly round the table. 'You were everything I'd ever dreamed of in a woman; soft, kind, like a kitten just graduated from the litter. So innocent, so trusting. . . .' His hand clenched whitely on the table edge. 'I couldn't believe that you actually cared for me, that——'

'You're forgetting something,' Lee reminded him woodenly when he paused. 'You were married at the time.'

'Yes, I was married.'

The explosive bitterness in his voice made Lee start, her eyes coming up to trace the features that were, and always would be, etched on her heart.

'You stayed married,' she pointed out in a small but persistent voice, and flinched again when Kelsey rounded on her savagely.

'Yes, I stayed married. What else could I do? I asked her for a divorce when I got back from San Francisco that time. That was the time,' he swung bitterly away from Lee's view of his distorted features, 'when she told me that if I ever left her she'd kill herself.' He came back into Lee's view, waving a dismissing hand. 'It was an idle threat, just as her promises of having a child at some future date were. And she didn't make it because she cared for me, loved me. She was a mixed-up woman, Lee, as different from you as night is from day. All she really cared about was being somebody, living in the best neighbourhood, feeling that people with less money were envying her. I don't know,' he ran his long fingers through his hair, cutting furrows through its thick blackness, 'maybe she'd always resented being the poor relation in Dorothy's family. Whatever it was, I knew that she was unstable, ready to blow her stack at any time. In her own way, she needed me.'

He pulled his chair forward and sat down again, his eyes bleakly fixed on Lee's. 'There were never any other girls, Lee, I swear it. My marriage was a wash-out almost from the start, but I never felt the need or the desire to have an outside relationship. Until I met you,' he ended heavily.

'And since?' Lee asked in a constricted whisper, unable to stem the flooding warmth within her when he shook his head and looked down into the coffee he had barely touched.

'There's been no one. I hadn't given up hope of getting a divorce when I heard that you . . .' his eyes lifted to hers, taking her breath away with the depth of pain reflected in them, 'that you'd married Fletcher Whitney. There didn't seem much point after that. Susan and I were together officially, but privately we went our separate ways. She had her—friends, and I had the island.'

Lee drew a long, quivering breath. No effort of imagination was needed to surmise that Susan's 'friends' had been of the male variety. Bitterness rose and tasted sour in her throat. What kind of a woman had she been, threatening suicide when her husband asked for his release, then condemning him to a solitary private life on this island while she took her pleasure with the man of the moment?

'She deserved to die.' The thought had barely formed in her mind before they were on her lips, and she gave Kelsey a stricken look.

'No one deserves that kind of death, Lee,' he came back, quietly sober. 'The strange thing is,' he went on thoughtfully, his eyes straying beyond Lee to the shaded side wall of the kitchen, 'I think she'd always expected to die in the same way as her parents. They were killed in a car accident, and she seemed to accept somehow that she would die that way too.'

A shiver bristled up Lee's spine. 'She couldn't have known that,' she reasoned. 'I mean, you were driving, not her. She couldn't have manipulated destiny so that the road would be slick with rain that night, although——' She broke off and bit her lip, wishing it was her tongue.

'Although?' Kelsey prompted softly.

'Well——' she hesitated, then plunged, 'You *had* been to a party that night, hadn't you?'

'If you're implying I was drunk at the time, you're wrong,' he clipped. 'I'd had no more than a couple of drinks well spaced. My wife had taken in her usual share, and that, combined with her unfounded jealousy of a woman I'd spent a little time with at the party, was why she——' It was his turn to break off, his mouth compressing to a thin line.

Lee stared at him in dawning comprehension. '*She* caused the accident, didn't she? It wasn't the rain that made the road slick, it was Susan who did it, wasn't it?' Her eyes grew wide as the realisation hit her. 'She manipulated destiny, didn't she, and made sure she died in the same way as her parents.'

'I'm not sure why it happened,' Kelsey said, his voice lowered to huskiness. 'All I know is that she grabbed the wheel and the car skewed across the road and ended up halfway down a cliff side. She was killed outright.'

'And you might have been too,' Lee breathed, horror at the thought deepening the blue of her eyes to indigo. 'Oh, Kelsey!'

'Would it have mattered to you?' He reached across the table and took her hands in his. Helplessly, she stared into the jet darkness of his eyes. This wasn't a time for prevarication, but. . . .

'I'd have wanted to die too,' she said simply, and felt the sudden crush of his fingers bruising her own.

'Why did you do it, Lee?' he begged in a voice made rough by emotion. 'Why did you marry a man old enough to be your grandfather? Didn't you trust me enough to know that I'd move heaven and hell to come back to you?'

Being on the defensive was something Lee was unaccustomed to, especially with Kelsey. For so long, she had nourished the hatred spawned by his seemingly cavalier treatment that she was lost in a situation where he became the accuser.

Her voice came out sharply, but lifeless. 'I trusted you enough to get pregnant by you. It was Fletcher who married me, not the other way round. I wasn't interested in his money, Kelsey,' she enunciated bitterly, 'but in providing a name for the product of a— what is it called?—a one-night stand.'

The pupils of his eyes contracted, then flared in disbelief. 'You had a child? My child?'

He read the answer in Lee's eyes, and his hands withdrew from hers suddenly and covered his face. Time stretched interminably, silence broken only by the harsh breaths Kelsey drew through his pinched nostrils. It wasn't a time for speech. What could she have said anyway?

At last his muffled question came. 'The child— where is it now? In San Francisco?'

The sorrow that had filled her then flooded back to her now as she said brokenly, 'I—lost the baby. At four months. I was already married to Fletcher by then.'

Kelsey drew his hands away from his face and stared at her with haggard eyes. 'You were expecting my child, yet Whitney married you?'

'Fletcher married me because of the baby, yes, but also because he had been my father's closest friend. He was fond of me, as I was of him.'

'How fond?' Kelsey asked harshly.

'He had been married for many years to a woman he loved,' Lee forced her voice to steadiness. 'He looked on me as the daughter they might have had but didn't. He gave me his name, his protection, his worldly wealth when he died. He—asked nothing in return.'

Pain shot through her when Kelsey's features seemed to disintegrate before her eyes. Yet she felt incapable of constructive action, drained of the corrosive poison that had filled her for so many years. She saw without feeling the ravaging effects of this evening's events on Kelsey's face, observed the deep glint signifying tears in the eyes he fastened on her.

'I don't know what to say,' he shook his head bemusedly. 'I think I owe Fletcher Whitney an apology for misjudging him all these years. But I can't give it to him, can I?'

No, he couldn't do that, she acknowledged silently. Yet Fletcher would be the first to take her happiness as his own. How many times had he told her, the wisdom of ages in his eyes, that love would come to her? The kind of love he had shared with his wife of more years than Lee had lived.

'You can give it to me,' she said tremulously through the resurgence of feeling infiltrating her limbs, her heart, her whole being. It seemed natural, right, when Kelsey rose and stretched out his hands to her, their supple warmth enfolding them as his arms circled her waist seconds later.

'I apologise,' he said without hesitation, his voice huskily constricted. 'To Fletcher, and to you. Mostly to you.' His eyes seemed to burn holes in the skin they raked closely over. 'If only I'd kept in touch with you, told you what I was planning . . . but I didn't, and all the regrets in the world won't alter that now. But I love you, Lee.' His hand brushed lightly through her hair and came to rest on her nape. 'God, how I love you! I thought I knew how much before, but when I saw you standing there against the window upstairs in the room where I'd planned you would be, it was as if I'd been born again into a world that was entirely new to me.'

Lee's hands reached for his shoulders, then caressed lightly up to where the thick growth of his hair started. 'I thought I'd planned perfectly too,' she whispered, 'but it didn't take long for me to figure out that hating you was something I had used for years to cover up what I really felt for you.' She reached on tiptoe to place her lips on the hard line of his jaw, allowing the pent desires of years to speak further for her, and Kelsey's arms grew tight round her, pulling her to the taut line of his fitly muscled body.

'We'll have other babies,' he told the shell outline of her ear, and she nodded dazedly.

'Yes.'

His mouth betrayed the same haste that prompted Lee's tilt of her head to meet the lips that wrought havoc with every principle etched into her. The only principle she would acknowledge now and for ever was the importance of the man she now held in her arms, knowing that his pulses beat in unison with hers. Her lips parted, took his in and thrilled to the throbbing warmth of his mouth on hers. The soft tips of her breasts were already hard when his fingers found them, her body pliant as it moulded itself to the taut curve of his hips.

'Does this mean you'll agree to marry me?' Kelsey nipped provocatively at her ear, 'or do I have to take stronger measures?'

'If you'll submit your proposal in triplicate,' Lee murmured, her lips yearning with shameless provocation, 'I'll consider whether Whitney's will benefit from such an alliance.'

Kelsey's head reared, his eyes pinpoints of flame as he demanded, 'Are you going to be my wife or President of Whitney Enterprises?'

'Can't I be both?'

'Do you want to be?'

'At this moment, no,' she returned frankly, her fingers smoothing the short hairs at his neck. 'But I know the time will come when I'll want to be part of what's going on. I love you, Kelsey, and I love your island and everything else that goes with you. But I'd hate it if I felt I couldn't do something else as well as being your wife.'

'Even if we have children?'

'Even so,' she returned steadily, not blinding herself to the fact that love for their children could never wholly replace her life as an independent business woman. Kelsey accepted on principle the fact of women in business, but how far would that liberal view stretch when it had to encompass his wife, children?

'Then,' he said, 'they'll just have to get used to a mother who commutes a lot to San Francisco.'

'But only,' she ran her fingers through the thick cluster of his hair, 'if their father commutes with her.'

A hard flame lit the inner recesses of his eyes. 'Let's leave it open to negotiation, shall we?'

'Yes,' she agreed, knowing even as she committed herself that nothing, nobody in the world would ever matter so much as this man did. He was her life, her love, the sum of all her parts.

Who could ask for anything more?

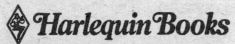

What readers say about Harlequin romance fiction...

"You're #1."

A.H.,* Hattiesburg, Missouri

"Thank you for the many hours of lovely enjoyment you have given me."

M.M., Schaumburg, Illinois

"The books are so good that I have to read them all the way through before being able to go to sleep at night."

N.Q., Newark, California

"Thanks for many happy hours."

M.L., Millville, New Jersey

"Harlequin books are the doorway to pleasure."

"They are quality books—down-to-earth reading! Don't ever quit!"

"A pleasant escape from the pressures of this world."

"Keep them coming! They are still the best books."

Harlequin Presents...

The books that let you escape into the wonderful world of romance! Trips to exotic places... interesting plots... meeting memorable people... the excitement of love....These are integral parts of Harlequin Presents— the heartwarming novels read by women everywhere.

Many early issues are now available. Choose from this great selection!

Choose from this great selection of exciting Harlequin Presents editions

Relive a great romance... with Harlequin Presents

Complete and mail this coupon today!

Harlequin Reader Service

In the U.S.A.
1440 South Priest Drive
Tempe, AZ 85281

In Canada
649 Ontario Street
Stratford, Ontario N5A 6W2

Please send me the following Harlequin Presents novels. I am enclosing my check or money order for $1.50 for each novel ordered, plus 75¢ to cover postage and handling.

☐ 99	☐ 103	☐ 109
☐ 100	☐ 106	☐ 110
☐ 101	☐ 107	☐ 111
☐ 102	☐ 108	☐ 112

Number of novels checked @ $1.50 each = $ _____

N.Y. and Ariz. residents add appropriate sales tax. $ _____

Postage and handling $ ____ .75

TOTAL $ _____

I enclose _____
(Please send check or money order. We cannot be responsible for cash sent through the mail.)

Prices subject to change without notice.

NAME _____
(Please Print)

ADDRESS _____

CITY _____

STATE/PROV. _____

ZIP/POSTAL CODE _____

Offer Expires February 28, 1982.   106563170